PRAISE FOR JACQUIE BIGGAR

Ms. Biggar has written an easy to read, heartwarming, sexy and funny, opposites attract hero and heroine that could walk right off the page and into your heart.

— AVONNA- THE ROMANCE REVIEWS

OMG!!! What an absolutely delightful book!Ms. Biggar is one of my favorite authors. Her wonderful ways of telling a story are just amazing and in the storytelling part, this novella does not disappoint.

— BARBARA

She's become one of my favorite authors and she knows how to capture her readers attention.

— JANE STRAUGH

CRAZY LITTLE THING CALLED LOVE

GAMBLING HEARTS- BOOK 2

JACQUIE BIGGAR

WAVEFRONT PUBLISHING

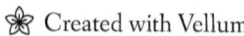 Created with Vellum

For my Family,
If not for your encouragement, I may never have strived
to become a writer.
Now, I can't imagine any occupation that could better
allow me to live my dreams.

Love ya always and all ways,
Jacq

True love stories never have endings.

— Richard Bach

INTRODUCTION

"I've missed you," he admitted, his free hand wrapping around the nape, under a heavy fall of hair the color of wheat at harvest time.

Her eyes slid closed, head lolling back on a slender neck. They opened into slumberous wells of gold. "You knew where I'd gone. I waited for you to come."

The hurt in her voice tore at his heart. If only it weren't so complicated. "Sophia..."

She shook her head. "It doesn't matter anymore. What's done, is done. I'm here now, cowboy. Are you going to kiss me, or not?"

His eyes widened and then a slow grin tipped his lips. That was Sophia—all sass.

"Well, yes ma'am. I reckon I am," he said with an exaggerated drawl. Then he leaned down and did what he'd been aching to do since she returned to the ranch —he kissed the girl.

Sophia's head swam, overloaded with sensations. The feel of a masculine chest against hers. The scents of hay and horse and man. The luxurious softness of his hair beneath her fingers, and the touch of his lips. Oh, God, that mouth. She'd dreamed of his mouth so very many times since she left. The way he groaned when she opened for him. The almost voracious quest to learn every centimeter of her mouth and what made her moan in return. They'd always been explosive together, whether in passion or fury, and it was the same now.

He muttered words she couldn't understand, his lips roaming her jaw, her ear, her neck, everywhere he could reach. She was just as desperate, her hands tracing the new lines on his face, the breadth of his shoulders, the molded muscles in his arms and back. He was the same as she remembered, yet different too, his body toughened by years of manual labor and an unforgiving Texas sun. If anything, it only made him more attractive, in the way of masculine men who worked hard and didn't give a damn what others thought. Rugged men.

She shifted, trying to edge closer, seep under his very skin if she could. His leg suddenly gave out. He cursed and broke away, bracing himself with a hand on Rex.

Embarrassed, worried, and over-sexed with no place to go, she crouched to get a better look at his knee. "This looks bad. You should get off of it before you do serious damage." When there was no answer, she glanced up, her eyes widening over the thick bulge in his jeans. She licked her lips nervously and met his whimsical gaze.

"Are you offering, darlin'?"

Five years and a degree in business management, yet one phone call could still leave Sophia Shaughnessy feeling like a rebellious child.

"Why are you the one calling?" she asked the bane of her existence. The functional silver clock radio on top the bookcase warned her to hurry up if she didn't want to get caught in the early morning New York City commute, but *his* voice had rooted her to the floor.

"Because your brothers wouldn't, that's why. It's time you quit the spoiled princess act and give them the support they need."

She literally saw red. Tony Morrison could get under her skin faster than a Texas tornado, and he'd cause just as much damage if she let him.

Pumpkin rubbed against her legs and mewed. Sophia turned the phone to speaker, set it on the counter and picked up the heavy tabby, holding her close for comfort. Pumpkin licked her chin, then settled into her arms with a purr that almost, but not quite, succeeded in drowning Tony's voice.

"You've had more than enough time to get over your snit. Now that your grandmother has passed..." he hesitated for a moment, "... Matt and Aaron have their hands full managing the property. They need you, Soph."

And what about you?

Silly question. Tony was too busy being mature and responsible to admit to such a base emotion as love. It had destroyed their relationship five years ago; she ought to be over him by now.

So how come one phone call and she was ready to drop everything to run back home if that's what he wanted?

She was pathetic.

"I have a life now," she said, scratching Pumpkin's tender belly. "I can't just leave at the drop of a hat."

She ignored her phone lying on the counter and wandered across the room to gaze down at the hustle and bustle of urban life in the big city. Taxis, distinctive with their bright yellow paint, zipped in and out of gridlocked traffic in well-rehearsed choreography, while people milled on the street like ants at a picnic. Further away, she could just see the treetops of the famed Central Park, providing a bright burst of green against the endless grey skyscrapers. It was true. She had a career, friends, a nice apartment. It wasn't the ranch, but most of the time she could convince herself it was just as good.

"I'm not asking you to give up your life," Tony said, his voice disturbingly clear in the silence of the room. "Just come home for a while. Your brothers miss you."

She swung around, angry at the condemnation in his tone. "I was there three months ago, why didn't they say something?"

"Consuela was upset you didn't stay longer after the funeral."

She couldn't, it hurt too much. The ranch held too many memories. Every room reminded her of the woman who'd taken three scared, lonely children in and raised them as her own after their parents—and her husband—died in a plane crash. She'd given them love and a home and Sophia had repaid her grand-mother by not even being there when she was needed the most.

To say goodbye.

Pumpkin squirmed and Sophia set her pet down,

taking a moment to clear her head. When she rose, her decision was made.

"Tell Matt I'll be there next week."

Heaven help her. It wasn't bad enough she'd be living with her grandmother's ghost, her very-much-alive ex-boyfriend would be there too.

*T*ony signaled and slowed the crew cab to turn onto ranch property, hyperaware of the quiet woman hugging the passenger door. Sophia had changed from the fun-loving, impulsive girl she'd been five years ago. This woman was a stranger.

"Happy to be back?" he asked to break the silence.

She glanced his way, then rolled down the window allowing the early summer air to flood the cab. "Calving season over?"

Honey blond hair fluttered in the breeze, distracting Tony with a visceral memory of its herbal scent. His fingers tightened on the steering wheel. "Yeah, a month ago. Four hundred and twenty-two, up this year.

"Good," she murmured, tucking the runaway strands behind her ear. "That's good."

So civilized. Anyone listening would never guess they'd once made plans to marry and have six kids together. She'd always wanted a large family like her own, while he... he'd wanted her to be happy.

Look how that turned out.

"Any trouble getting time off from your job? What was it again, advertising?"

That earned him a glare. "Promotions and marketing manager. And yes, it was a lot of trouble. Not that you care." She opened her handbag and dug around until she found what she was looking for—a small bottle of prescription pills.

Tony frowned. "What are those for? Are you sick?" He couldn't control the concern in his voice. Hard not to worry after her grandmother just died of cancer.

She unscrewed the lid, tipped a couple pills into her palm, and screwed the lid on before swallowing the drugs dry. She dumped the bottle back in her bag and came out with a pair of dark sunglasses that she perched onto her nose. "How are my brothers?"

Okay, then. He let it go... for now. "As well as can be expected. Aaron came home from college, and Matt is coping. He's lucky, he has Cassandra and their new baby to keep his mind off... well, you know." He shifted in his seat. He didn't know why he was uncomfortable referring to Madeline's death. It was a fact of life and something every cowboy was familiar with, but this was the ranch's chatelaine—the heart of the Shaughnessy family—and the loss was keenly felt by everyone.

Sophia nodded and cleared her throat. "I can't wait to see her, I'm going to spoil her rotten." They shared a smile before things got awkward and she turned away from him. "Not far now."

Not far enough. Soon she would be surrounded by her family and he would once again be the outsider. He pulled over and stopped in a cloud of dust.

Sophia stared at him, her mouth open. He would have smiled except for the tension pervading the cab. He threw the truck into park and turned in his seat. "Talk to me, Soph. You're killing me here."

Her expression softened, and a glimmer of the old Sophia appeared before she put the lid on it, snapping her mouth shut and withdrawing as much mentally as physically.

"There's nothing to say. I'm here for a couple of weeks to help my brothers and then I'm going back to New York. You can have the ranch, Tony. It always was more important to you than I was."

He swore under his breath. This was an old argument between them. Whenever she didn't get her way, she brought up his loyalty to the Shaughnessys. It drove him crazy then, and it wasn't much better now.

"You are the most irritating, stubborn woman I've ever met." Frustrated, he took his cowboy hat off and rubbed his scalp. "Why can't we ever have a normal conversation?" he asked, determined to come to some sort of understanding before they reached the ranch.

She stared at the strap of her purse she was mutilating with her fingers. "There's too much history between us to be friends, Tony." She glanced up, her expression hidden behind those damn glasses. "Let's just agree to stay out of each other's way and leave it at that, okay?"

No, it wasn't *okay*. Nothing about this situation was *okay*. Unfortunately, he'd burned his bridges years ago, the least he could do was grant her this—though it was tearing him up inside.

He straightened and shifted the truck back into gear. "Yeah, sure, princess. Whatever you want." He stabbed the gas with his foot and took off down the road like his tail was on fire.

Sophia held onto the door handle and swallowed the sobs fighting to escape. She'd known coming home was going to be hard, but not this bad. It was easy to fool herself from a thousand miles away she was over Tony. That she could help her family and go back to her life in the city with barely a scratch—instead it had been hardly an hour and she was already bleeding from the inside out.

How was she going to hold it together in front of Matt?

Her oldest brother had been her hero ever since their parents died and they came to live with Grandma Maddie. He'd taken over as a father figure and practically raised her and Aaron. He'd asked about her and Tony at the funeral, but she'd assured him it was over. Because it was.

Her goal was to help get the ranch out of the red, straighten the bookkeeping, then go back to New York and bury her sorrows in work. She played with the bottle in her purse. It had been a mistake pulling it out in front of Tony, but she'd been jittery. Hopefully, their argument would keep him from mentioning it to Matt, she didn't want to worry him. The doctor had assured her if she was careful, the beta-blockers would be temporary, she just had to learn to control her stress levels.

The field of wheat running alongside the road swayed in the wind, the sun's rays turning the stems to gold. A windmill perched on top of a knoll, its blades lackadaisical in the light breeze. She and Tony had often ridden out to the quiet spot. Hours spent holding each other, talking, kissing, and later on, making love.

Tony Morrison introduced her to passion and no man since had lived up to his lessons.

She risked a sidelong glance at his strong hands as he guided the steering wheel around a bend in the road. A shiver of longing rode up her spine. Why did she have to fall for the one guy she could never have?

3

The moment the pickup pulled up, the courtyard was flooded by people—a sea of laughing, crying faces. The family housekeeper, *Tía* Consuela, her round face alight with love hurried toward them, skirts flapping around her ankles. Matt followed close behind, his arm around Cassandra, who had their precious baby daughter, Pippa. Aaron stepped out from the shade of the portico, his ready smile making an appearance, but the stress of the past months apparent in somber eyes and the creases furrowing his forehead. For a moment, Sophia fancied she even saw Grandma Maggie travelling along the flagstones in her wheelchair, a soft, welcoming smile lighting her cherished face. The turbulent emotions building throughout the journey home—really, since learning of her grandmother's death—rose up to choke her, the ready tears turning everyone into a water-colour painting.

"Pull yourself together," Tony said, his voice a harsh intrusion. "Your family has been through enough, they don't need to be worrying about you right now."

Shock froze the tears and cast a layer of ice over her heart. No one talked to her that way. Who did Tony Morrison think he was? She lifted her chin and swiped the moisture from her eyes with trembling fingers. Her move to open the door and escape the insufferable jerk was unsuccessful—he'd locked her in!

"If you don't unlock this door I'm going to scream, and trust me, you don't want that. My brothers think you can do no wrong, Mr. by-the-book Morrison, but you and I both know you're nothing but a wannabe, isn't that right?" She glared at him, both hands on the door now as if sheer will could blast it open. "You've been insinuating yourself into this family for ten years or more. Never take a holiday. Barely go to town. What are you hiding from?" *Or who?* She ached to know more about his life, but he'd always kept a closed book attitude to his past. Another reason they'd split up; without trust, love withers.

His eyes were cold, remorseless. "This isn't about me. You've acted the spoiled little rich girl for long enough. Your precious ranch is in trouble. Those

people out there—" he glanced over her shoulder, "—
need your help and I plan to make sure you step up to
the plate. They've coddled you your whole life, it's past
time you grew up and faced reality." He unclicked the
lock. "Now, quit pouting and paste a smile on those
pretty lips. Your family is waiting."

His words cut deep, revealing truths she didn't
want to accept. Was she really that heartless? Different
times played out in her head, a litany of moments
where a whine or a cry had garnered the results she'd
wanted. Matt had worked endlessly to be father and
mother to her and Aaron, and she'd lapped it up. It
embarrassed her how much she'd taken for granted
when their loss had been as keen as her own. Worse—
they'd been nearly teenagers when the accident
happened—where she'd been scared and confused,
they'd known the depths of despair.

"Tony..." she hesitated, lost for words. He'd
changed in the past five years, grown colder. Distant.
But then, so had she. "I'm sorry. I shouldn't have said
those things. You've always been here, and my family
appreciates your loyalty. Truly."

His shoulders hunched, and resignation filled his
expression. "Go now. We'll have time to talk later."

Her heart felt as though it was tugged in two direc-
tions. She hated to leave things the way they were with
this man who meant—used to mean—the world to her,

but beyond the window her family beckoned with open, loving arms. And she was weak.

She nodded, her throat too tight for words, and opened the door allowing the outside chaos to rush into the cab with something of a relief.

"Sophia, my baby girl, you came home. Praise the Lord, you came home." *Tía* Consuela was the first to greet her, enfolding Sophia into her warm embrace. Tears fell unheeded as she wrapped her arms around the elderly woman and hung on, feeling like that five-year-old girl all over again.

"I've missed you so much," she whispered, gulping on the sobs.

"I know, *pequeña*. It is going to be all right. You will see." Consuela patted her back. "Your family, they need you."

"Damn right, we do. It's your turn to muck the stalls." Aaron grinned, hands on hips and cowboy hat pushed back on his curly blond head. "And that horse of yours is plumb miserable."

Sophia gasped. "Aaron Michael Shaughnessy, you take that back. Cleopatra is the smartest, sweetest horse on this ranch, and you know it, too." Cleo. She couldn't wait to take her for a ride. Feel the wind caressing her skin. Breathe fresh and clean air free of carbon monoxide. Tomorrow. First thing tomorrow she would saddle up and revisit her old haunts.

"Don't I get a hug?" Matthew said, laughter softening his handsome face. "Come say hi to your niece."

Sophia stared at her brother, babe in arms, and a strange ache spread through her chest. He'd make an amazing dad. Pippa would never lack love and support, or a strong shoulder to lean on when life threw her a curveball. The ache turned to determination. Matt loved this ranch, heck, they all did. If there was anything she could do to save the land for his little girl, then Sophia owed him to try.

She kissed *Tía* Consuela's papery cheek, smiled into the kind brown eyes, and went to greet her niece.

4

*T*ony raked fresh straw over the floor, made sure there was plenty of water and hay in the feed trough, then led the big black bugger into his stall. Goliath was amendable today, possibly because Matt had taken him for a good run yesterday before his sister came home. The seventeen-hand beast gave a whole new meaning to the word cantankerous. But he sure produced some handsome foals. Matt's new breeding program was gaining attention from as far away as Kentucky, and they'd even sold a couple of colts up north in Canada. It would be a few more years before they'd built up a strong enough herd to make serious money, but it was a start.

He latched the stall and rested his arms on the half-door. "There, are you happy now? Clean digs, girlfriend waiting outside, and everyone at your beck and call—I wish I had a horse's life."

Goliath listened, ears flickering, intelligent brown eyes focused on Tony. His head jerked with temper, silvery mane rippling and black coat glistening, then let out a strident cry before dismissing the man to munch hay.

Tony grinned. Nothing like a horse with attitude. He dug in his pocket and found the apple he'd been saving for a snack later. "Here. How about a peace offering?" He held it in his open palm and waited for the black brute to take the bait. "C'mon. I don't have all day, you know." Tony's chest warmed with affection at the almost ticklish feel of soft lips as the big animal delicately sampled the apple. "You're not so bad," he murmured. "We're alike, you and me. All we want is to be left alone, right?" Except, that wasn't true. Goliath had Matt, and he... well, he had anonymity.

He gave the stallion a pat on the muscular neck, then continued down the length of the corridor, nodding to other employees cleaning stalls. Rico stopped and leaned on his shovel, waiting for Tony to draw even.

He tipped his hat back on curly black hair and stuck a piece of straw in his mouth. "Is it true the boss's sister done come home?"

Tony bristled, though the question was innocuous enough. "What's it to you, Juarez?"

Rico straightened—half a head shorter, lean and lanky compared to Tony's boxer-wide shoulders— the man was like a bantam rooster with his chest stuck out. "I's just asking, Morrison. No need to go staking your claim. We all know you had a thing for Sophia. You might want to remember some of us were here before you, though. We're friends, that's all."

The nearby horses had picked up on the tension, snorting and restless in their stalls. Tony cursed under his breath, aware he owed the other man an apology. He rarely lost his temper, not that you'd know it the way he'd been acting for the past few days.

"Didn't get my coffee this morning," he said, by way of excuse. "She arrived yesterday. The family is right glad to have her back—however long she stays."

Rico moved the straw from one side of his mouth to the other before he allowed the starch to ease out of his stance. "*Tía* Consuela will be over the moon, she thinks of Sophia as a daughter."

That's right, Rico's mother was Consuela's sister. On a ranch the size of this one, entire generations of employees were often born and raised on the land. Tony himself had arrived here as a teen and worked his way up to foreman. They were a close-knit community and he was an idiot for getting his back up.

"So, you think she's going to leave right away?" Rico asked, and the pensive light in his dark chocolate eyes was enough to tweak the strings on Tony's patience.

"I don't know. Why don't you ask her? I'm not her babysitter."

"Ask me what?"

Both men turned at the sound of Sophia's voice. Tony's heart gave a little bounce in his chest at the vision standing before them. No one wore blue jeans the way she did. They lovingly hugged long, lithesome legs and red leather cowboy boots that could happily walk all over him and he wouldn't mind a bit. Some kind of frilly white shirt was tucked into those oh-so-dangerous jeans and covered with a wide Concho belt. A white felt cowboy hat perched jauntily on blond curls, and Abalone earrings and a teardrop necklace completed the ensemble. Normal barn wear.

Rico's straw fell out of his mouth and Tony clamped his own lips shut. One man drooling over the princess was enough.

"It's not even noon yet, what are you doing out of bed?" The moment he said the words, he wished them back. His mind filled with visions of her stretched out on snowy white sheets, nothing between her skin and some voyeuristic rays of sun seeping between the blinds and bathing her body in strips of light and shadow. He wondered if she still preferred to sleep in the nude.

Rather than taking offence, she simply smiled and strode forward to give Rico a hug. "It's been a lot of years since I could stay in bed all day. This girl works for a living now." She took a step back but retained her hold on Rico's shoulders. "Look at you, all grown up." She laughed at his outraged look. "*Tía* Consuela said you'd be here. I just had to come down to see my old friend. It's been too long."

Rico shot Tony a triumphant look, then grinned, his hands going to her waist. "It's about time you came home, *pequeña*, we have a wedding to plan."

Tony's fists curled, and going by the startled glances he received, a snarl might have been involved. His jaw ached from gnashing his teeth together and it felt as though the tendons in his neck were bulging.

Sophia gave him a nervous peek from under the brim of her hat, then used laughter to escape Rico's grip. "That was a children's game, Rico Juarez. And besides, Consuela has already told me all about your bevy of girlfriends. I hardly think you've been pining for me."

Maybe Rico hadn't been. Tony banished the thought the moment it entered his head. He might have dreamed of her return for a lot of years, but he was over it now. There was no way he could ever compete with big city lights, nor did he care to. She'd made her decision and he'd accepted it. All that was left was to teach his traitorous heart the new rules.

Sophia lightly flirted with Rico—as they'd done all their lives—and pretended not to watch every move Tony made. She absolutely didn't notice his tough farm hands closing into fists when Rico grasped her waist, or sense the tension emanating from his powerful body as he watched the two of them acting like frisky colts. She'd feel guilty, except the big jerk should know there hadn't been anyone but him for her since she'd reached puberty.

Damn him.

"I thought I'd take Cleopatra out for a ride," she said to Rico, making a conscious effort to ignore Tony's glower. "Do you have time to join me?"

"Sure." Rico nodded. "Just give me a few minutes to finish these stalls, *bueno*?"

"Weren't you supposed to exercise the yearlings today?" Tony growled. "Just because the princess deigned to visit, doesn't mean the ranch is on holiday. Get to work, Juarez."

Rico bristled. "I can do that later, they aren't going anywhere."

Tony took an aggressive step forward and Sophia hurried to step between the two men. "Stop it," she hissed. "It's my fault, I wasn't thinking."

She turned and forced a smile for Rico. "I'll meet you later and we'll catch up. It's been too long." She squeezed his arm in reassurance. "See you at dinner?"

Rico glared at his boss, then gave a slow shrug and dragged his attention back to her. "Yeah, sure. It'll be like old times, *sí*?"

Sophia saw his intentions in the mischievous glint of his eyes. She braced herself for the fallout as he leaned in and gave her a big, smacking kiss on the lips before jauntily wandering away with a tip of his hat. She'd get even with him, the tease.

She glanced up at Tony and cleared her throat, subduing the instinct to rub suddenly sweaty palms on her pants. "I didn't mean to create problems, I know this is a working ranch." That much was true, anyway. She'd tried so many times to insert herself into the business, to be a valued member of the team, but her ideas were brushed aside as the dreams of a young idealist. After a while, she'd given up trying.

Tony met her gaze and sighed. "I probably overreacted. I tend to do that a lot around you," he admitted. Sophia didn't have time to enjoy the warm glow his words wrought, before he added, "But you should know better than to come down to the barns dressed like that. You're distracting my men."

She wasn't sure which rose faster, outrage or pleasure. She went with outrage, it was safer. "I'm wearing blue jeans, they're hardly haute couture. And most of your men have known me since I was knee-high to a grasshopper, you're exaggerating my appeal. Now if you'll excuse me, I'm going to see my horse. At least she doesn't judge me."

She'd stomped past three stalls, the horses within staring at her with inquisitive eyes, before Tony caught up to her. "It's been a long time since you've been on much of a ride, I don't like the idea of you going out alone."

Sophia huffed out a strangled laugh. "I was born on this ranch, I'm pretty sure I know my way around it. Besides, it's your own fault I don't have a companion, you got rid of him, remember?"

Tony grabbed a couple of bridles on their way past the tack room. "That idiot would be too damn busy showing off to protect you," he snapped. "And I wasn't worried about you getting lost so much as getting bucked off and, if you were lucky, landing on that delectable keister. I'll go with you."

"No." She swung around to face him. "I want a fun, *relaxing* ride. You'll just mess with my Zen."

"You want to go, princess, then I go too. End of story." He opened the stall for his bay and entered, mumbling sweet nothings to the horse while he swung the bridle over the gelding's head.

Oh, yay.

att sighed and threw his pen on the mahogany desk. His grandfather had imported it from India as an anniversary present for his wife, Madeline. She'd chastised him for wasting all that money, but it'd been obvious she'd loved the beautiful piece of furniture. Although, not as much as she adored her burly husband. Joseph had brought her to his father's hacienda as a blushing sixteen-year-old bride. Times weren't easy in the fifties, but they'd persevered and built the ranch into a thriving business by the time Matt's dad was old enough to take over. Then cattle prices dropped, and they'd been forced to take that plane trip to Denver—they'd never returned. Matt lost his parents, his grandfather, and his childhood that fateful day. And if he didn't find a way to catch up these back taxes, he was going to lose the ranch. His family's legacy.

A light knock on the closed door jerked him out of his reflections. Cassandra entered with Pippa perched over her shoulder, a burping cloth protecting her clothing as she gently patted their daughter's delicate back.

"I thought we'd find you here," she said, sharing a sympathetic smile with him over the cluttered desk. "Are we interrupting?"

Matt rose and side-stepped the desk so he could kiss his girls. "Never. I needed a break, anyway." He cupped Pippa's dark head and breathed in the fresh, baby powder scent. "Just finished her bath?"

Cass nodded, her turquoise eyes rich with love and laughter. "She's definitely a Pisces, she loves water. You should have seen the fuss when I took her out, fists flying, legs pumping, and that cry... I would've put her back in, but she was already turning into a prune!"

Matt smiled. Their daughter was *gaining personality*, as Grandma Maddie would have said. She seemed content now, her skin rosy and eyes half-closed as she nuzzled her mother's neck. His heart overflowed, and he had to breathe deep past the constriction in his chest. He'd come from a warm, affectionate family, but the depth of love he had for his wife and daughter defied words. How could he tell them they were in danger of losing everything?

He could go back to gambling, but at best, that was a long shot. Meanwhile, the new horse breeding program, while netting results, would take years to build up a sustainable cash flow. With cattle prices the way they were, and the drought global warming had gifted them with, he couldn't see a way out of financial disaster within the next two or three years—if they could hold out that long.

"What's wrong, Matt?" Cass grasped his hand as he turned away, anxious to keep his disquiet from transmitting to his family. "You've been preoccupied for days. I thought you'd be happy now that Sophia has come home."

He sighed and sank into one of the twin leather wingback chairs. "It's not that. Of course, I'm glad she's here, it's where she belongs. I don't know why she had to go across the country to get some fancy-assed degree anyway."

Cassandra squeezed his fingers, then let him go to open her shirt and maternity bra and shift the babe into her arms. She sat in the opposite chair and nudged the tiny cheek until Pippa latched onto a breast. They were quiet for a moment, content to watch the miracle that was their child.

"She's so perfect," he whispered.

Cass looked up at him, her expression serene. "She is," she agreed. "Now, tell me what has you upset."

Matt hesitated, unwilling to ruin the moment. "We've had an offer for the ranch. It's a good one. I'm thinking of accepting."

Her forehead crinkled. "What are you talking about? Why would you even consider such a preposterous idea?" The baby fidgeted, picking up on the tension. Cass held her finger close to Pippa's tiny hand and the baby grasped it, settling down to feed again. "You know I support you, whatever you decide, but..." she met his gaze, "... I think this should be a family decision. It's too much for you to handle on your own."

She was right. Aaron and Sophia deserved a say in their future. He just wished it hadn't come down to this.

6

*S*ophia patted her horse's thick neck, overjoyed to be back in the saddle. She tipped her head and closed her eyes, the sun a warm benediction on her face. Instead of the non-stop congestion caused by city buses, cars, honking horns, and grim-faced pedestrians, all she could hear was the creak of saddles, the swish of grass against their horses' hooves—and peace.

At least until she was reminded of her companion.

"I'm surprised you still ride so well."

She frowned and glanced over her shoulder at the brooding man following her trail. "I told you I'd be fine. I don't need a babysitter."

"You could have fooled me," he muttered. His gaze slid down her back, then jerked up to her face.

"Regardless, we better not go too far, or you'll be sore tomorrow."

Some imp of mischief had Sophia standing in her stirrups. "C'mon, Morrison. Race you to the water hole." She leaned low over Cleo's neck. "Let's show him, girl. Go!" Startled, Cleopatra reared, then took off at a gallop, her long strides eating up the ground. The pounding hooves and heaving breaths from the powerful animal between her thighs made it impossible for Sophia to hear how close the competition was, and she refused to give him the satisfaction of looking. Cleo's mane flayed her skin, but the thrill of the chase kept her focused on the goal, a crystal-clear pond nestled in a stand of oak trees. The wind brought tears to her eyes, or maybe it was the tsunami of memories swamping her as they raced across those flats. Picnics with Grandma Maddie, trips to Hidden Valley with her brothers and their father, Matt and Cassandra's wedding at the cabin—and Tony.

Always, Tony.

He'd held her when she'd cried after her parents' accident, and picked her up after a particularly bad fall at a barrel racing competition. He'd given Cleopatra to her for her sweet sixteen birthday and kissed her gently on the lips. And a year later, he'd shown her what it meant to be a woman.

She caught movement off her left side and raked

her heels along Cleo's flank, asking her horse to give a final push to the finish line, but it was not to be. Tony's big bay inched alongside until they were neck and neck, both horses' heads stretched out, hooves pounding, and air see-sawing in and out of their gallant bodies.

Suddenly, Sophia lost her lust for a win. She pulled up on the reins, slowing Cleo and allowing Tony to sail by like they were standing still. Cleopatra snorted and shook her head, flecks of foam flying into the air. "I know, girl, you were amazing. You could have beaten them." She reached over and patted the slick neck. "Sometimes, it's better to let them think they won. Pride is a tricky beast." She should know, pride ruined her and Tony's relationship the first time. His and hers.

Tony glanced back and hauled up on his reins, turning his horse around to trot back to them. "What's wrong, are you hurt?" he demanded, his worried gaze tracking over her body.

She smiled and shook her head. "We're fine. I just decided to let you win, that's all." Her heart flip-flopped at the sudden glint in his sky-blue eyes, a stark contrast to skin burnished a dark copper brown from the Texas sun.

"You *let* me win, did you?" he taunted. "Maybe the city girl knows she doesn't have what it takes."

"Whatever floats your boat, Morrison." She prodded Cleo and they soon entered the coolness of the glade. The pond beckoned, a clear blue-green with ferns surrounding the bank and water lilies floating among the reeds.

Sophia dismounted and allowed her horse to step into the water for a drink, the rocky bottom solid beneath the animal's hooves. Tony joined her, his hand going to her elbow when she slipped on the bank.

"Careful there, Sunshine, or you'll be going for an unplanned swim."

His fingers tightened, sending shivers of awareness up her spine. Maybe a cool dip wouldn't be such a bad idea. "Thanks," she murmured. "Beautiful here, isn't it?"

"Yes." His voice had deepened, and she could feel his gaze on her rather than the surrounding grove.

"I wasn't fishing for a compliment, you know." She took a hurried step away and almost went down again. His touch kindled painful memories she didn't know how to handle. "How have you been, Tony? Are you seeing anyone?" Sophia cringed. Why did she ask him such a personal question? It wasn't like she *wanted* to know about his love life, for pity's sake. God, she was an idiot.

He let go of her arm and strode to the horses, loosening their girths for drinking. When he was done, he leaned over Cleo's back and stared at her. "There's no one right now. What about you? Have a rich city boy waiting in the wings?"

She snorted and shook her head. Cowboys were an arrogant bunch. Look at him now, hat tipped over wavy tobacco brown hair, blue eyes that rivaled the crystal clarity of the water, and powerful shoulders used to a hard day's work. Yes, he was the polar opposite of most of the men she knew in New York City with their fancy briefcases and cellphones plastered to their ears, but that only made him more attractive.

"What have you got against people earning a living with their minds instead of their hands, Morrison?" She sat on the bank and tugged off her boots and socks so she could dip her toes in the water. Oh yeah, that felt good. The shade provided by the towering oaks kept the pond on the cool side, just perfect for hot summer days. It was only June and already her shirt was sticking to her back. She'd gotten used to the more temperate east coast weather since she'd been away. When Tony didn't answer she looked up to see him staring at her bare feet as she played in the shallows. He had such an intense look on his face she froze, wondering if there was a snake cozying up to her through the tall grass.

"What's wrong? Tony Morrison, if I'm about to get bit, you better darn well do something about it!" She wanted to jump and run with every fiber of her being, but she knew better. Sudden movements triggered attacks. Her brothers had taught her the rules of the bush—it didn't mean she wasn't scared though.

"Huh?" he asked, jerking his gaze to her face. His neck flushed brick red and he lowered his arms, swatting the horse's haunches to get her to move aside. He dipped a cloth in the water, wrung it out, and wiped his face and neck before looking at her again. "I was just surprised you wear nail polish now, you never used to bother with that girly crap before."

She ducked her head to hide a smile. Suddenly this day just got a lot more interesting.

7

Tony eyed the temptress teasing him with sidelong smiles and pink toenails, and wondered if he'd made a fatal error in judgement. If not for his belief in her ideas he may not have completed the phone call that instigated her return to the ranch. She was dangerous to him. She made him want things between them to be different—but, they weren't. She was so far out of his league they may as well be from different galaxies. He'd come a long way, thanks to her family's generosity, but the past was a gossamer web waiting to trap those he cared about, and he couldn't afford to take any chances. Not with Sophia.

"You just going to stand there, cowboy?"

Her sultry voice reached deep inside and tugged on dreams and wishes he'd worked hard to stifle. It made him angry, resentful of the power she wielded over him. It'd been five years, when would this attraction fade?

"We should go. Your brothers will be wondering where you are." His fidgeting with the reins transmitted to the horses. They danced sideways, sending water up in a wide arc that covered his jeans. He cursed and jumped out of the way. "Look what you made me do now," he said, swiping at the wet stains.

"Me?" She giggled. "Cleo obviously thought you needed cooling down."

He got a mental picture of the horse picking him up by the scruff of the neck and dumping him in the pond, and grinned. "I guess it could have been worse." He dropped the reins to ground-tie the troublemakers and joined Sophia on the bank. "Guess we have to wait awhile, I don't want to explain this to the crew." He waved at his wet crotch.

She glanced down, then slowly lifted her gaze to his, the smile dying from her lips. "No," she murmured. "We wouldn't want that."

Great. Now the pants weren't only wet, they were tight.

"Tell me about city life," he urged, anxious to remind himself why kissing her would be a very bad idea. "Is it all you thought it would be?"

She shrugged and avoided his gaze. "Yeah, sure. It

took some getting used to—especially the noise—and I love the shopping." She shot him a teasing smile that pinched him in the chest. She was definitely a clothes horse. Her brother was as much to blame for that as anyone. He'd often returned to the ranch from one of his big gambling excursions laden with gifts for his siblings; clothes and shoes for Sophia, books and electronics for Aaron. Guilt for being abroad so much, Tony figured. Problem was, it created expectations the average Joe could never hope to compete with.

"School was fun. I learned a lot about business management and advertising."

"I bet the partying didn't hurt either," Tony muttered, hating the thought of her amid all those frat boys.

She punched his arm.

"Ow," he said, rubbing the affected area. "What did you do that for?"

She gave him a mulish glare. "I didn't care about those guys, and well you know it. When are you going to get it through your stubborn head it was you I loved, you big moron."

Well, when she put it that way.

Then the rest of her words sank in—loved, as in past tense. As in, you had your chance and wasted it, you idiot.

"Anyway," she said after a pregnant pause, "once

I received my degree, a company on the west side hired me to reenergize their ad campaign, and after that, as they say in the business, they were sold. Offered me a full-time position, corner office, pension plan, the whole nine yards." She gazed across the pond. "I've been there almost two years already. Crazy, right?"

Extremely.

Tony had tried to be happy for her when she'd left for university, but he'd expected her to return home with her fancy degree and then things would go back to normal. That never happened. Month after month he'd listened for any word of what she was doing, and when she was coming home. Then Consuela mentioned something about her new boyfriend, a lawyer, and Tony realized it really was over between them. He'd briefly considered leaving the ranch but couldn't bring himself to break the connection with the only family he'd ever known.

Or at least, the only one that mattered.

"So, you're happy?" he asked, a sucker for punishment.

She lifted her knees, her toes digging into the Texas loam. "Of course, what's not to like? I have a fabulous apartment close to work, a job that keeps me on my toes, and an active nightlife. It couldn't be more different from here."

Was that melancholy he heard in her voice? "Listen, if you want to come back..."

Her laugh was harsh. She picked up a stone and heaved it at the water, watching as it broke the surface like a mini explosion before disappearing beneath ever-widening ripples. "You'll what? Find something to keep me busy so I don't get in the way of the real work?" She jumped up and shoved bare feet into her boots, forgoing socks. "No thanks. I've been there, done that, have the trophy. It's time to go, *Tía* Consuela needs me even if you don't."

What just happened?

Tony rose and dusted off his jeans, keeping a wary eye on Sophia as she stomped toward the horses. They shied a bit at her abrupt approach but were too well-trained to go far. Even in the midst of a temper, Sophia was gentle with her horse. She rubbed Cleo's forelock before tossing the reins over her head and reached for the pommel.

"Sophia, wait," he ordered, exasperated. Why could they never have a civil conversation?

The glance she sent him was laced with the same frustration he was feeling. "I'm glad you called me to help, Tony, but we both know Matt will never take me seriously. And I can't stay where I'm not wanted." She swung into the saddle. "I'll do what I can. See you back at the ranch."

Cleo kicked up a whirlwind of dust as Sophia wheeled her mount around and took off as though demons were chasing her.

How was he going to convince her to stay? Because she was wrong about one thing—he wanted her.

8

*S*ophia sat at the kitchen island—leg swinging from the bar stool as she'd done since she was a child. Consuela pulled pieces off a big mound of pimply dough, rolled them between dexterous hands into marble-sized rounds and dropped them three at a time into greased muffin tins. Her pull-apart rolls never lasted long and had caused more than one argument at the dinner table.

"What has that pretty face looking so glum, *pequeña?*" Consuela finished a pan, set it aside to rise, and slid another batch into one of the kitchen's double ovens. She wiped her brow as she straightened, leaving a floury streak on her cheek. "Don't tell me Matthew is giving you grief already. Goodness gracious, you barely got here."

Sophia poked at the dough and promptly had her

fingers tapped. "Sorry," she grinned, "habit. No, I've hardly seen Matt yet. Or my darling niece, for that matter. How are he and Cassandra managing as new parents?"

Consuela smiled. "They are learning to grab naps whenever the little one does. Pippa is a good baby. Always happy, that one."

Envy reared its ugly head. Matt and Cassandra had it all; someone to hold when life throws hard knocks, a precious child, and the security of a home. She was glad her brother had found true love, no one deserved it more than him. But it exaggerated all that she was missing in her quest of a worthwhile career. Sometimes, being an independent woman wasn't all it was cracked up to be—she was lonely.

"I brought some frilly outfits home for Pippa, I hope they fit her. I'm not used to buying baby clothes, but I couldn't resist when I saw them."

Consuela gave her a knowing glance. "Your time will come, just you wait and see. You're young yet, babies take a lot of work."

"And there's the small matter of a husband," Sophia interjected, rising to pour each of them a tall glass of iced tea. "Unless you know of another way."

"Don't get sassy with me, missy. Just because I devoted myself to this family instead of getting married, doesn't mean I never thought about it. It's perfectly natural to want your own child, that's all I'm saying." Consuela climbed onto a stool, her wide girth and short legs making the action a chore.

Sophia frowned. She'd selfishly never considered *Tía* Consuela's personal dreams before. She couldn't remember a time without the grandmotherly house-keeper. She was the worker bee of the family; caring first for three scared, lost children, then later for Grandma Maddie as the cancer attacked her body. In between all that, she'd kept this monstrosity of a house immaculate and cooked for the Shaughnessys as well as their staff. They would have been lost without her.

She grasped her aunt's soft, slightly greasy hand, and squeezed. "Why have you never talked to us about this? Who was he, *Tía*? This man who made you think of babies. I sincerely hope we didn't have anything to do with whatever happened. I'd hate to think you gave up your happiness for us."

Tears turned Consuela's eyes espresso dark. She gave a tremulous smile and shook her head. "No one made me stay, *pequeña*. You and your brothers, you were always good kids. Your momma and daddy were so proud of you all. And then came that fateful, horrible day…" She fished in the deep pockets of her apron, came up with a tissue and gave her nose a vigorous wipe. "You were a little bitty girl, and with the terrible loss to your family, you may not have comprehended it at the time, but your parents and grandfather were not the only ones on the airplane that day. Miguel was your Grandpa Joseph's pilot. We were to be married that summer, but of course, the Lord our God had different plans for our loved ones." She made the sign of the cross on her breast. "*Señora* Madelaine had to set her pain aside to care for her precious babies, and I found comfort in easing her burden with the day to day chores."

She took a long drink from the frosty glass of tea. "It wasn't easy for any of us, but your family became my family. We do what we have to, *sí*?"

Sophia nodded and got up from the stool to check the buns in the oven. In truth she needed a moment to digest what she'd learned. All these years they'd never known. It was tradition to take flowers to the graves on the anniversary of the accident. Now that she thought about it, Consuela had always joined them, but stayed back once they arrived at the graveyard. Could she have been visiting her fiancé's plot? Grandma Maddie should have told them.

She set the hot pan on the stove with a clatter and turned, slapping the gloves together. "Why didn't you or Grandma tell us? We could have helped."

Consuela slid off her stool and hurried over to hug Sophia. "You *are* a help. Every day you and your brothers make me proud." She kissed Sophia's cheek, then gave it a pat. "Enough now, the past is the past."

She turned and bustled back to the waiting dough, ripping off another chunk with practiced fingers. "Tell me how your morning ride went with *Señor* Tony." Her eyes twinkled. "He is a handsome man, no?"

"No. Yes. I mean, I guess!" Sophia sputtered, her cheeks hotter than the buns she'd just pulled from the oven. She shook her finger at Consuela. "Get that thought right out of your head. We're friends, that's all. *Just* friends."

Consuela shrugged, tossing a round blob into the pan. "Sure honey, whatever you say. Now come and help me with this dough. These buns aren't going to make themselves, you know."

That was it?

Where was the big third degree? The '*Tony's a nice boy, you could do worse*' speech? He was nice. And handsome. And aggravating. And impossible to forget.

Sighing, she joined her aunt at the counter.

9

*T*ony froze on his way into the hacienda's large kitchen. He'd been planning to sweet-talk Consuela out of a picnic lunch and maybe see if Sophia would join him—not now.

Friends.

The death knell to a relationship. '*I really like you, but as a friend.*' He should have known. He'd waited too long. If he was smart he'd start looking for another job. It was time to move on, there was nothing holding him here anymore.

Suddenly, he felt weak at the knees and braced his back against the wall for support. His chest grew tight, a vise stealing the breath from his lungs. His head thunked the wall as the hallway swam. He blinked rapidly in an effort to clear his vision. Maybe he was having a heart attack.

Inside, he knew though. It was Sophia.

The thought of never seeing her again, never holding her in his arms—it destroyed him. He'd been deceiving himself, pretending an altruistic motive for bringing her back to the ranch when all along he'd been holding onto the foolish notion she'd take one look and fall in love with him like she'd done as a too-tempting teenager. He almost wished he'd taken advantage of her infatuation and married her then. But, it wouldn't have been fair to either one of them. And that decision had cost him the girl.

"Hey, what are you... Whoa, man, you better sit down before you kiss the ground." Aaron hurried forward, his boots clunking on the tile, and grabbed Tony's arm. "You're whiter than the ghost stallion that's been helping himself to our herd."

He glared at Aaron. Any louder and the guy may as well do a Facebook post and tell the world about it. "Get me outta here," he growled. Aaron jumped at the harsh tone before tucking an arm around Tony's waist and attempting to lead him into the kitchen.

Oh, hell no. "Not there. I need to lay down," he improvised. Though maybe he might really need to after this. He'd been through less stress at his yearly prostrate exam.

They managed an escape to the den without detection. Aaron helped him to the settee, then strode to the bar and poured a shot of scotch into a tumbler. Tony accepted the offer but did nothing more than cradle the delicate crystal in his rough working man's hands. Talk about having the point driven home. She was the princess, while he was nothing more than the dirt beneath her shoes. Even less if she ever found out about...

"It works better if you drink it." Aaron slouched in a matching butter-soft leather chair, his own glass resting on his knee. "Wanna talk?"

Tony gave him a disbelieving glance. "Thanks, but I'll pass."

"Suit yourself. I don't understand why guys have such an issue expressing themselves. It helps relieve tension, if nothing else."

Tony took a drink, needing the slow burn to eat through his frustrations. "You planning to become a shrink, or something?"

Aaron's laugh was tinged with bitterness. "Why? Just because I offered some good advice? Consider it the benefit of being the middle child, I'm the peace-keeper around here."

Well, that was true. Matt tended to lay down the law and Sophia liked to argue over every decision. Good thing they had Aaron as the voice of reason.

"I'm sure they appreciate your guidance, but I don't need any help. I think it's just a touch of the flu."

"Yeah, sure. The Sophia bug," Aaron said. "I heard her in the kitchen. Since you were doing everything short of hogtying me to keep from dragging you in there, I'm going to guess you two are quarreling. Again."

Tony scowled. "It had nothing to do with Sophia, okay? Matter of fact we went for a ride the other day and had a nice talk." Until she rode off and left him without a backward glance, anyway.

Aaron sat up, enthusiasm lighting his eyes. "Did she tell you about New York City? The shows, the lights, the action? Man, I stayed with her for a couple of weeks last year and loved it."

Oh, oh. Tony didn't like where this was heading. Matt would be devastated if another Shaughnessy split for the city. He needed all hands on deck, not another member of his family jumping ship.

"Aaron," he started, then hesitated. It wasn't his place to tell the younger man what he should or shouldn't do.

"I know." Aaron slung the rest of the contents of the glass down his throat with barely a grimace and jumped to his feet. "A guy can dream though, right?" He walked over to the bar to refill his glass and shrugged when Tony shook his head at the offer of more. "I'm stuck on the ranch for the foreseeable future. I've come to terms with it, but it doesn't mean I have to like it. Sometimes I wish I was the youngest, like Sophia, and could do whatever I wanted."

Tony wasn't sure that was true. The Sophia he remembered had dreamed of turning the ranch into a guest retreat where visitors could get a taste of ranch life by taking part in different activities such as a cattle drive, trail riding, branding—all the things that made dude ranches a favorite with vacationers looking for adventure and luxury in one sweet package.

"If you feel that way, you should talk to Matt. Maybe he can help."

"Yeah, I don't think that's a great idea. He has enough to deal with right now. And besides, Pippa needs her uncle." He set the glass down, drink unfinished, and strode for the door. "I better get back to work. The boss is a tyrant. I'll let him know you're not feeling good, shall I?"

Tony shook his head but didn't rise yet. He needed a moment to get his head on straight. "Nah, I'm good. See you out there."

Aaron raised his hand in salute and then he was gone, closing the door in his wake. Tony leaned back and stared at the ceiling. The thought of leaving the Shaughnessy household really did make his head swim. Somehow, he had to get past Sophia's rejection and carry out the plan he'd started by calling her home.

Bringing their family together again. He owed it to them.

10

Sophia was in the ranch office going over the books when her brother walked in. The sight of Matthew stirred conflicting emotions in her breast. Pride; he was a handsome man, after all, and she'd always hero-worshipped him. He also made her tense. She ached for him to see her as strong in her own right. Not another responsibility, but as an asset. Someone he could count on, one of the team.

Not a child.

"Hey, kiddo, how's it going?" He headed straight for the coffee machine, added a pod to the chamber and snapped down the lid. Soon, the heavenly scent of Arabica beans filled the air. Sophia inhaled the aroma, peeked into her own empty cup, and sighed. Matt glanced over and raised a brow in query. "Want one?" he asked.

"Sure, thanks." She'd get the next round. If he stayed. "Where's Cassandra and the baby?" Sophia had spent yesterday afternoon visiting her sister-in-law and holding Pippa while she slept. If all babies were that quiet, she didn't see what the fuss was about.

"Resting. Pip was fussy last night, we didn't get much sleep." He yawned and took a long drink of his coffee while waiting for hers to finish brewing. "Still take yours black?"

Pleased he remembered, she nodded. Empathy rose. Maybe she didn't know as much as she thought she did. It wasn't like she'd had the opportunity to babysit much growing up. There weren't many kids on their ranch. Or at least, ones younger than her. And therein lay the problem. Everyone had treated *her* like a baby, and she'd hated it. Especially Tony Morrison.

"Thanks for offering to look over the finances. I have to admit, accounting is not my forté," he said, returning her cup filled with steaming deliciousness to the desk.

"I'm happy to help." She hesitated, then grabbed the bull by the horns and plunged on. "I've been working on something for a while now that I think could make a difference for the ranch. There's a big upsurge in the tourism industry, Matt, and we aren't taking advantage of that." She frowned when he started to shake his head. "You're not even going to hear me out?"

He sighed and slumped into the club chair on the other side of the desk. "This is a working farm, Soph. I told you that years ago when you first came to me with the harebrained idea of turning this place into some sort of silly dude ranch. I couldn't see it working then, and I don't see it doing any better now."

Sophia had had ideas rejected by her professors and even corporate heads, so why did it hurt so much now? If she didn't love the ranch, she'd raise her hands and walk away. But, there was a deep compulsion inside to see this dream through. She just had to convince Matt to trust her instincts. *No problem.*

"Look, Matt..."

Aaron strode in without knocking, a belligerent look in his eyes. "Figures. You guys plan a Shaughnessy reunion and don't invite the life of the party, shame on you."

Sophia rose and circled the desk to give her brother a welcoming hug, frowning at the scent of alcohol on his breath. "Well, I for one am glad you're here." She glanced over her shoulder at a glowering Matt before smiling into Aaron's face, willing him not to jump to conclusions. "I've barely seen you since I came home. Have you been avoiding your favorite sister?"

His shoulders relaxed. A wry smile twisted his lips

below a sandy moustache. He ruffled her hair and turned away to help himself to the coffee. "You're my only sister, goofball." He blew on the cup before taking a sip. "And no, I haven't been avoiding you, work calls. It's branding season, if you remember now that you're a city gal."

She was starting to hate that term. Yes, it had been her decision to leave, and yes, she sometimes regretted it, but there was no denying the experience had helped her grow into her own skin. To gain some much-needed confidence, out from under her brothers' intimidating shadows.

Determined to make her point now that she had a captive audience, Sophia returned to her side of the desk and sat down, suddenly nervous. She cleared her throat. "Umm, I was just telling Matt about a possible source of revenue for the ranch. Got a minute?"

Aaron glanced at Matt then shrugged. "Sure, this should be interesting." He took up a corner of the wall, well-worn boots crossed at the ankle, a brass buckle glinting from the belt of his blue jeans.

Matt leaned forward, his expression earnest. "Sis, you know I value your input, but I really don't want a bunch of city slickers wandering around my ranch getting into who-knows-what. We already have the new foal program up and running, as well as our cattle and feed sales. We'll get through this hiccup, it'll just take time, that's all."

"Cut her some slack. You haven't even heard her sales pitch yet, have you?" Aaron shot her an encouraging look. "The least you could do is hear her out. And by the way, it's *our* ranch, asshole."

Sophia grimaced. He wasn't helping matters with his aggressive behavior. And what was up with that, anyway?

Matt rose and stalked toward the door. "I don't have time to argue with you. *Our* ranch won't run itself."

Oh no. She didn't mean to cause dissention. She'd been trying to help, but as usual, she'd only made matters worse.

Aaron stepped in front of the door, his stance pugnacious. "You're always running away. First when our parents died, and then later, when Grams got sick. When are you going to admit you don't have all the answers, big brother, huh? When are you going to quit trying to run our lives?" He gave Matt a shove, forgetting he still had a cup of coffee in his hand. It tipped across Matt's chest, leaving a dark stain and total silence.

Sophia bit down on the fist she'd raised to her mouth, her horrified eyes not fully comprehending what just happened. This wasn't right. Her family was close. They'd always been the three musketeers—together no matter what.

"Matt..." Aaron reached out to his brother, his hand shaking. "I'm sorry. I didn't mean..."

Matt brushed him off, his expression stark. "It doesn't matter. I have to go." He opened the door, then hesitated, his back to them. "I was doing what I thought best. Obviously, I've failed." He strode out without closing the door, leaving a patch of sunlight on the floor where he'd stood.

Sophia's eyes welled. All because she'd tried to push her stupid ideas onto them again. When would she ever learn?

"I'm going to town. Don't count on me for dinner tonight, okay?" Aaron set the now empty cup on the coffee bar and followed Matt out the door.

And then there was one.

11

Tony rode into a courtyard bathed in the rich indigo of an evening sky. After a long day, he looked forward to a cold beer and a hot shower, in that order. The clip-clop of his horse's hooves on the cobblestones echoed in the hush of dusk's peaceful solitude. This was his favorite time of day, the cooler air caressing overheated skin, animals grazing quietly in the fields, and families gathering to share the evening meal. It was bittersweet and poignant, a time when he was part and yet apart from his deepest desire. A family to call his own.

He didn't have to guide Rex to the barn, the horse chewed his bit and led the way, anxious for his nightly feed. Tony reached down and gave the satiny neck a rough caress. "I promise an extra ration of grain, you did good today. The hills hide those calves too well, sometimes."

His dismount was a tad awkward. He'd twisted a knee chasing a cow through the brush and it was making itself felt. He gathered the reins and limped into the barn, adding ice packing his knee to his list of things to get done. A form separated itself from the shadows halfway down the aisle—Sophia.

He frowned over the acrobats doing flips in his chest. "What are you doing out here all alone?"

She ignored that. "You're hurt."

Tony glanced down at his leg, faintly surprised at the tight fit of his jeans around the knee. "It's nothing. I'll put some ice on it soon." Rex shifted, forcing him to place weight on the leg and he gave an involuntary wince.

Sophia moved closer, her brow furrowed. "That looks painful, you'd better sit down."

He didn't need her sympathy. "Don't worry, Princess. It won't stop me from doing my job." He opened Rex's stall, grateful he didn't have to walk any further until Sophia was gone. "Rex is hungry, so if you don't want to get stepped on, I suggest you move aside." He might sound rough, but he placed his body between her and the big animal, aware one misplaced kick could kill.

Rex followed him into the stall like a pet dog, reins

trailing and shoes shuffling over the clean straw bed. Tony unbuckled the bridle and tugged it over his horse's head, straightening the long black forelock before removing the saddle.

He glanced up as Sophia entered the stall, carrying a steel pail filled with oats, barley, and crimped corn. "Thanks," he muttered, wishing he could stay mad at her. It would be so much easier.

Rex snorted and tried to push her out of the way so he could get at the feed, but she just laughed and nudged him, dumping it into the trough.

"Be a gentleman, now. *Unlike your master*," she whispered, a mischievous sparkle in those incredible honey-brown eyes.

He could be a gentleman. There wasn't much call for politeness on a ranch filled with hard-working cowboys, but he knew his manners and how to treat a lady. Even if he was rusty.

"So, um... what are you doing wandering out here all alone when your family is probably anxious to spend time with you?" He hefted the saddle over his shoulder and started for the stall door.

"I needed some time to think. It's quiet here. Nice, you know?"

The gloominess in her voice drew him up short. She'd only been here a week and already those brothers of hers were making her miserable. He ached to kick their asses. He'd never stood up for her all those years ago; that wasn't going to happen this time.

Even if it meant his job.

He cleared his throat. "I'm just going to take this to the tack room, will you stay?" He held his breath until she nodded, releasing it in a short, relieved gust of air. "Okay, good. Be right back."

The sore knee was all but forgotten as he hurried down the corridor to the dark tack room and set his gear down, intending to return later to inspect and polish the expensive leather. On the way back, he stopped and grabbed a bale of hay from the loft, the twine cutting into his fingers as he lugged it the short distance to Rex's stall. At first, he didn't see Sophia and his heart sank, but then she peeked out from under Rex's neck, a curry comb in hand.

"Oh, good. I was hoping you'd remember the hay. It doesn't bother you anymore?" she asked, resuming the long, sure strokes over the animal's back.

"Hmm?" Tony murmured, his own back quivering to feel her touch.

"Hay fever, did you find something to control it? I remember Consuela making cold compresses for your poor eyes. Funniest thing, considering you worked on a ranch, and all."

Tony set the bale down and cut the ties, the stiff rectangular cube suddenly expanding like an overweight man undoing his belt after a big meal. "Yeah. Finally gave in and went to the allergist in Houston. She gave me a steroid spray and decongestant eye drops. Don't think it works any better than Consuela's home remedies though."

Rex shifted to get better access to the feed and suddenly he and Sophia were on the same side of the big beast, the animal between them and the stall door. The lighting was muted, intimate, hushed. The only noise came from the crunch, crunch of the horse shredding the hay between strong, square teeth.

Sophia studiously ignored him, concentrating on the hypnotic sweeping motion of her hand brushing the chestnut coat to a dull gleam. Tony watched for a time, bemused by how this petite woman could hold a big moose like Rex in thrall with nothing more than the sweet touch of her fingertips.

He reached out and grasped her hand, stilling the movement. She looked at him then, the same sensual awareness shimmering in her eyes that fired his blood. He brought her around to face him, the brush dropping unheeded to the floor.

"I've missed you," he admitted, his free hand wrapping around her nape, under a heavy fall of hair the color of wheat at harvest time.

Her eyes slid closed, head lolling back on a slender neck. They opened into slumberous wells of gold. "You knew where I'd gone. I waited for you to come."

The hurt in her voice tore at his heart. If only it weren't so complicated. "Sophia..."

She shook her head. "It doesn't matter anymore. What's done, is done. I'm here now, cowboy. Are you going to kiss me, or not?"

His eyes widened and then a slow grin tipped his lips. That was Sophia—all sass.

"Well, yes ma'am. I reckon I am," he said with an exaggerated drawl. Then he leaned down and did what he'd been aching to do since she returned to the ranch —he kissed the girl.

Sophia's head swam, overloaded with sensations. The feel of a masculine chest against hers. The scents of hay and horse and man. The luxurious softness of his hair beneath her fingers, and the touch of his lips. Oh, God, that mouth. She'd dreamed of his mouth so very many times since she left. The way he groaned when she opened for him. The almost voracious quest to learn every centimeter of her mouth and what made her moan in return. They'd always been explosive together, whether in passion or fury, and it was the same now.

He muttered words she couldn't understand, his lips roaming her jaw, her ear, her neck, everywhere he could reach. She was just as desperate, her hands tracing the new lines on his face, the breadth of his shoulders, the molded muscles in his arms and back. He was the same as she remembered, yet different too, his body toughened by years of manual labor and an unforgiving Texas sun. If anything, it only made him more attractive, in the way of masculine men who worked hard and didn't give a damn what others thought. Rugged men.

She shifted, trying to edge closer, seep under his very skin if she could. His leg suddenly gave out. He cursed and broke away, bracing himself with a hand on Rex.

Embarrassed, worried, and over-sexed with no place to go, she crouched to get a better look at his knee. "This looks bad. You should get off of it before you do serious damage." When there was no answer, she glanced up, her eyes widening over the thick bulge in his jeans. She licked her lips nervously and met his whimsical gaze.

"Are you offering, darlin'?"

She snorted and rose quickly, fanning her cheeks. "In your dreams, Morrison." Suddenly in need of some cool air and a clear head, she ducked under Rex's neck and escaped her confinement. "I better go. Are you going to be okay to get home?"

He stared at her over the horse's broad back. "Sure. Don't worry about me, I'm a big boy."

Sophia smirked. He had that right.

12

*S*ophia awoke the next morning to a pleasant surprise. She'd voiced concerns to Cassandra about the poor cat she'd left at a friend's house, and her sister-in-law had somehow made arrangements for Pumpkin to be shipped to the ranch.

"Oh, Cass, I don't know what to say," Sophia blubbered, her face buried in her pet's ginger fur.

"Not me, it was Matt," Cass insisted. "I mentioned you were worried about your cat and he made it happen."

Whether it had been done out of guilt or not, Sophia was grateful. She'd adopted Pumpkin not long after moving to the city. She'd been so lonely, and the orange kitten cowering in the corner of the pet store window had captured her heart.

"I hope she'll get along with Chewy." She set the

cat down and let it explore the large den, her attention caught by the painting that hung over the massive stone fireplace. Grandma Maddie was beautiful in a Spanish lace gown. Grandpa stared at her like he couldn't believe his good fortune. They'd shared many happy years together—until the plane crash.

"I'm glad the painting is back in the den. It suits this room."

"Want some advice?" Cass asked, her blue-green eyes warm with sympathy. "It's not your fault you'd moved to the city and weren't able to get home in time to say goodbye to your grandmother. Stop feeling guilty. She wouldn't want you to be unhappy."

If only it was so easy.

Her grandmother's spirit lingered in the chair she used to rock in by the fire. The brass candlesticks standing stately on the mantle, a gift from her husband on their anniversary, and the shelves of books. Sophia smiled, remembering the many hours Grandma Maddie had spent reading bedtime stories to her grandchildren.

Bittersweet memories.

Pumpkin brushed against her legs. Sophia scooped up her pet and cuddled her close, the soft purring a comfort to her bruised soul.

"I know you're right," she admitted. "Maybe it'll get easier, now that I can say a proper goodbye." She hadn't even been to the family graveyard since the funeral. *Tomorrow*, she promised herself. She'd take a bouquet of Grandma Maddie's favorite roses and spend some time visiting not just her grave, but those of her parents and grandfather as well.

"Where's Pippa?" she asked, rubbing Pumpkin's furry ear.

Cass glanced toward the closed double doors. "Consuela took her for a stroll. They should be back soon, it's almost feeding time." She pressed her palms to her swollen breasts. "I'm going to be sorry when she starts eating whole foods. It's a special feeling to give your baby nourishment from your body. And Matt enjoys the extra cup size, too." She laughed.

Sophia smiled to cover her envy. The older she got the louder her biological clock ticked. The problem with that was it took two—unless she went the in-vitro method.

Cass tipped her head quizzically. "What are you thinking?"

"Is Tony seeing anyone?" Sophia blurted, then covered her mouth, her cheeks on fire. "Never mind, it's absolutely none of my business." What was she, a teenager?

Cassandra reached over and ran gentle fingers over Pumpkin's silky fur. "Pretty cat, looks well cared for." She met Sophia's gaze. "No. He did for a while after you left, but it wasn't serious. There's only ever been you, honey."

Sophia's heart stuttered. She must have squeezed the cat too hard because she let out a warning yowl, jumped out of Sophia's grasp, landed with a soft plop on the sofa, and then scrambled to the floor to disappear from sight. "I don't know what to say. He was such a big part of my life, it took a long time to recover. I'm not sure I really have."

And wasn't that the most telling of all?

"If you don't mind my asking, what happened between you two? I thought you'd be getting married right after me, and then..."

"I was gone."

Sophia paced the room. How to explain her dissatisfaction, her frustration not only with Matt, but Tony, too. "The problem with being the youngest in a family of overachievers is that no one wanted to listen to my ideas." She dropped into the twin to Cassandra's chair, and wrung her hands. "I felt invisible, you know? And Tony... I thought he would stand up for me, be the one person on my side, but that's not how it worked." She sat back, stared at her grandparents' wedding picture. "They were a unit." She nodded to the painting. "I don't think I ever heard them disagree. Whenever Grandpa left the house, Grandma Maddie would see him to the door and they would kiss each other, then say, '*See you later.*' Not goodbye, see you later. Is it so wrong to want a relationship like that for myself?"

Cassandra stood and leaned down to give her a hug. "No, honey. There's nothing wrong with that at all."

13

The Shaughnessy graveyard sat on a grassy knoll west of the hacienda. A giant Sycamore tree stood sentinel in the center of the picket fenced area and provided shade for Sophia as she kneeled next to her grandmother's headstone.

In Loving Memory of
Madeline Shaughnessy
May 17, 1935 - September 10, 2010
Wife, mother, grandmother
Gentle of Heart

She brushed trembling fingers over the words, tears blurring her vision. "I still can't believe you're gone. You were my rock for so long, what will I do without you?" She sniffled, then gathered the flowers laying on the grass beside her and set them carefully in the glass vase to the left of the headstone. A stone angel with wings outspread perched on a pillar to the right, her face turned to overlook the homestead. Grandma would like that, a deeply religious woman, she'd never tried to push her grandchildren into her beliefs. They'd attended church with her on Sundays, and after that, it was up to them whether they said nightly prayers or read from the scriptures.

But Sophia remembered Grandma Maddie's Bible. A worn black leather cover had protected thin parchment-like pages rimmed with gold and dog-eared with age. She'd kept it nearby, often leafing through the pages with a serene smile that drew the children close, especially Sophia. She'd loved listening to the tales of David and Goliath, Jonah and the Whale, and Cain and Abel, but her favorite was Noah. It was hard to imagine the faith it took to build an ark in the face of ridicule, load it with animals, and then find yourself cast out to sea for forty days and forty nights before following a dove to dry land.

Blind faith was something she had a hard time accepting.

Faith hadn't brought her parents home. It failed to protect her grandmother from the disease that ravaged her body. Nor had it helped to keep what was left of her family together. Look at them now; Matt and Aaron could barely stand the sight of each other, and neither trusted her enough to give her a chance.

"What can I do?" She begged for some of her grandmother's wisdom and heard the shrill cry of a stallion in reply. Startled, she jumped up and whirled toward the sound. A horse paced just beyond the fence, dark eyes flashing and muscles rippling under ghostly white skin.

He was beautiful.

She'd heard the rumors of a stallion roaming the wild country, but this was the first time she'd ever seen him. Her brothers said he had a harem a hundred strong and guarded them fiercely. He took her breath away. Pride showed in the tossing neck and prancing steps.

He knows he's king.

His nostrils flared, scenting danger. He snorted and wheeled away, racing for the hills like a streak of lightning.

A horse galloped across the valley, its rider low over the animal's back. Tony skidded to a halt and vaulted over the fence, leaving his horse ground-tied and panting.

"Are you okay?" he demanded, grabbing her by the

arms and crushing her against his chest. "Dammit, you scared me to death."

Tony's heart pounded louder than the horse's hooves and he held her so tight she could barely breathe, but she didn't mind. Not really. She closed her eyes and pretended that just for a minute all the misunderstandings disappeared, and they were a couple madly in love. Her cheek rested on his shoulder, lips an inch away from his lean jaw, and all she could think was, *kiss me*.

"God, Sophia, you could have been trampled to death." He gave her a little shake, then grasped her face in his hands. "That horse is a rogue. He's stolen some of our top mares, and keeps them on the move. The men swear he's a ghost *bruja*. I wasn't kidding, you might have been seriously injured."

She could see his lips moving, but it wasn't fear she was feeling. Exhilaration, anticipation, expectation, yes. Frustration, too. Didn't he have the same overwhelming compulsion to sweep away the past and let passion dictate their future? They'd already tried the sane, logical route. She was damn tired of working to prove herself. She just wanted to... be.

"Are you going to kiss me?" Sophia demanded, interrupting his tirade. She almost smiled at the stupefied look he gave her. She'd shocked him. It was about time he realized she wasn't the malleable girl he'd let leave. She'd returned older, wiser, stronger. And she knew what she wanted.

She leaned forward, a scant few inches separating their mouths. His lips were hard at first, forbidding. That's okay, she was up to the challenge. Without allowing their bodies to touch anywhere other than his hold on her face and her hold on him, Sophia set out to prove they belonged together. She teased the corner of his mouth, little nibbling bites and soothing licks. Then, she did the same with the other side, ignoring the softening of his lips, the searching kisses designed to make her lose her mind.

He let her play for a while, his hands moving to drag her hips close. Then he let out a strangled growl and took over, the hard slant of his lips forcing her mouth open, so he could taste and take and plunder. Now it was her heart pounding like that of the racing stallion. her blood rushing through her veins and throbbing in her ears. Alive. She felt more alive in this instant than she had in years. This proud, stubborn man was her soulmate, she was lost without him.

Tony was going down for the third time. He'd tried, dammit he'd truly tried to give Sophia space. Let her decide her future, follow her dreams. It had torn him apart to let her go the first time, but she'd been too young, innocent. Unaware of her place in the world. It wouldn't have been fair to tie her to him, give her a child. The thought of his baby growing beneath her breast raised something wild and uncivilized within. He wanted to beat his chest and haul her off to his cave. Hold her there until she never wanted to leave. But, he couldn't.

Quite simply, she meant too much to him to allow her to ruin her life.

He lifted his head and put some space between them, the cool air a sharp contrast to his overheated skin. Her eyes were still closed, and that delectable mouth made a little mewling sound that damn near cancelled his good intentions.

"Sophia, stop," he growled. "We need to talk." Her eyes flickered, an adorable frown marring the creamy perfection of her forehead. She took a step back, and he felt the loss keenly.

"Why do you always do that?" she asked, resignation chasing shadows across her face.

"What?" he asked, afraid of the answer.

"Hide every time anyone gets too close." She reached out to touch his cheek, then let her hand drop. "I'm tired of playing this game, Tony. You have to know how I feel about you, I've never made it a secret." A sad smile touched her lips. "The ball is in your court now. What are you going to do about it?"

He stood there long after she'd left the family graveyard, the wind erasing the footprints she'd left in the sand and wondered if he would ever be brave enough to take a chance on love again.

14

*W*hen Matthew heard how close the wild stallion had come to the house, he was enraged. "That damn horse is dangerous. What if it had been Cassandra and the baby? I want that animal captured." He smacked the desk in the ranch office, glaring at Sophia.

She glared right back. "I'm fine, thanks for asking."

He straightened and frowned down his slightly crooked nose—Aaron had tripped him when they were kids and he'd busted it. "Don't be ridiculous. I can *see* you're fine, or I would have been just as worried about you. Why does everything have to be an argument with you?"

Is that what he thought?

Maybe she did bristle more than necessary, but her

brothers were larger-than-life, how else could she make sure her voice was heard?

"I don't think he meant me harm," she said, offering an olive branch. "He was magnificent, Matt. Remember the stories Grandpa Joseph told us about the phantom horse of Hidden Valley? Do you think this could be him, or maybe a descendant?"

He shrugged. "I don't know, but he's getting too brave for his own good. I was willing to allow him his space if he stayed out of my way, but he's stolen a couple of expensive mares and now, with you... He's gambling with his freedom."

"Another piece of ranch history gone," Aaron grumbled, half under his breath. He crossed his arms and slouched in a creaky wooden chair.

"What did you say?" Matt scowled, his brows a dark slash across his forehead.

Aaron pushed to his feet and Sophia was startled to see he towered over Matt by at least three inches, or more. When did that happen?

"Stop fighting," she shouted, startling them into silence. "What is going on with you two?" She pointed to Aaron. "You used to follow him around like he was a superhero. When did that change?"

Truthfully, they'd both been her heroes. Matt, the protector, and Aaron, the adventurer. They might not have always gotten along as kids—after all, they were *boys*—but she couldn't have asked for better guardians.

She sighed. "Look, this isn't solving anything. We're the custodians of this ranch, we need to work together to keep it in the family." She looked at Matt. "For Pippa, and any other Shaughnessys that happen to come along. Isn't that what you want?"

Matt nodded and sank into his chair behind the desk—his rightful spot as the eldest son. "Of course, it is. I think the stress is catching up to us, that's all." He gazed up at Aaron. "Right, bro?"

Aaron traded a loaded glance with him, then gave a gruff laugh. "Yeah, sure. What else could it be?" He returned to his chair. "Anything for the ranch."

Sophia was less than satisfied with his laconic answer but wasn't willing to chance calling him on it. Aaron seemed to have developed a hair-trigger temper while she'd been away.

She turned to Matt, curious about the new horse program. "What made you get into a horse breeding enterprise, isn't it risky?"

Aaron snorted. "Gambler by profession, did you forget?"

No, but obviously he didn't appreciate it was mostly *because* of Matt's gambling they still had a home to argue about. Matt had spent years traveling the world's poker circuits rather than where he longed to be, home on Balmoral. He'd traded peace for prosperity—until he met Cassandra and lost his heart and gained a bride.

"I didn't have a choice, and you know it," Matt snapped. "I've apologized until I'm blue in the face, what more do you want from me?"

"Apologized for what?" Sophia was bewildered. This wasn't like her family at all. She'd never known them to be antagonistic before.

Matt waved an impatient hand at his brother. "Ask him. He's got all the answers."

"Well, it's better than having no answer," Aaron was quick to respond. He looked at Sophia, an almost pleading expression taking over his handsome face. "A big-name developer wants to buy a section of our land. He plans to turn it into a subdivision for city folk looking to escape the jungle and relax in the countryside." He leaned forward again, his face intent. "He's offering enough to pay off our debts, Soph, and still have a tidy nest egg. It's too good to pass up, but big brother here," he glared at Matt, "won't even think about it. Instead, he's decided to spend more money we don't have on this *stupid* breeding program."

Matt flipped open a folder lying on the desk and twirled it around, so they could see. "Have you looked at the price of a Thoroughbred? They're used for more than racing. There's fox-hunting, show jumping, dressage, polo. It's a booming enterprise, one we'd be stupid to ignore. Look at these numbers. It might take a little longer than your ideas, but our ranch will remain in Shaughnessy hands. I promise."

Sophia stared at the spreadsheet filled with her brother's hopes and dreams, a riot of emotions battling in her breast. Instead of working together, as her great-grandparents had done when they homesteaded this land, the three of them were attacking the problem from different perspectives. And they were becoming enemies in the process. Suddenly, her vision of a fancy dude ranch seemed farther out of reach than ever.

ony wasn't one for baring his soul, but a little helpful advice was needed if he planned on healing the distance between the Shaughnessy siblings. He tapped lightly on the door leading into the spacious kitchen at the hacienda and waited for the faint, "*Hola,*" from the other side before turning the ornate brass knob.

Entering Consuela's kitchen was like entering the gates of paradise to a single guy who could barely cook a can of beans without burning them. He was hit with the scents of garlic, tomato and rosemary, mixed with burn-your eyes peppers and onions. His mouth watered.

"Are you making my favorite dish, Consuela?" he teased, smiling at the aging cook.

She looked up from stirring a deep cast iron pan

steaming on the gas stove and blew a wisp of still-dark hair out of her face. "If you mean chicken and three cheese quesadillas with my homemade secret recipe for salsa, yes. You're just in time, *Señor* Anthony."

He glanced around, relieved to see they were alone. "You know I can never say no to your cooking." She was the only one who ever used his full name, but he didn't mind. She was the nearest to family he had, other than the Shaughnessys.

"Why are you skulking around my kitchen in the middle of the afternoon," she asked, turning off the stove and setting the wooden spoon aside.

He hurried to take the pot holders and lift the heavy pan. "Where to?" He carried it to the silicone mat she pointed at on the long butcher-block island. "This chicken smells amazing, what did you put in here?"

"If I told you I'd have to *keel* you," she answered, only half-joking, and smacked his fingers when he snuck a piece. "Get out of there, you'll ruin dinner," she chided.

Tony patted his flat stomach. "Can you blame a guy? I've been eating my own chow for too long."

She smiled. "Tsk, tsk, poor man. If you weren't so stubborn, you could be eating with the family—as you should." She poured a mug of steaming coffee flavored with just a hint of cinnamon and slid a still warm sticky bun on an earthenware plate in front of him. "This is a new recipe, try it."

When a woman asked him to do something, he did. The first bite filled his mouth with the combined flavors of brown sugar, butter, cinnamon, and a bun that literally melted on his tongue. He closed his eyes and groaned. "You are a magician," he muttered around another bite.

She laughed, but a rosy blush climbed her cheeks. "And you are a rapscallion. How is it no young woman has captured you yet?"

Tony's enjoyment of the simple treat disappeared. He set the plate down and turned away to ostensibly wash his hands—in reality he needed a moment to marshal his thoughts. Sometimes, he wondered what he was waiting for, too. He'd dated off and on through the years—had even been serious about one woman whose parents worked for the Shaughnessys—but she wasn't Sophia. Once he'd given in to his attraction for the too-tempting teenager, there'd been no going back. The only thing he'd been able to do was damage control. He just never realized she would take his heart with her when she left.

"It is Sophia," Consuela said, reading his mind. "You still love that child, don't you?"

Tony swung around, ready to deny her allegations, but the sympathy shining from her dark eyes caused the words to ball up in his throat. He grabbed a hand towel hanging on the stove and wiped his hands, then took a drink of fragrant coffee before acknowledging the truth.

"It's the reason I came to see you today." He sat on one of the bar stools lining the counter. "She's hurting, and I don't know how to help her."

Consuela nodded. "*Sí,* I have seen the sadness she wears like a too heavy cloak. I thought because of her grandmother's passing, but there is more, yes?"

Tony drummed his fingers on the counter. "She wants what's best for the ranch, they all do, but her brothers refuse to listen. It's creating friction between them, and I'm scared it will make her run away again."

Consuela patted his hand, stilling his fingers. "This is something they must work out for themselves." She gave him an encouraging smile. "*Señor* Matt is fair, no? He will take her words under advisement, just give him time."

Tony frowned. "What if there is no time? Sophia owns my heart. Even if things don't work out between us, I want her to be happy."

His words brought tears to the maid's eyes. "I love that child as my own. It has long been my fondest wish that she would marry a good man and make her home here on the ranch her great-grandparents built." She dabbed the moisture with a linen hankie. "You are that man, Anthony."

He shifted uncomfortably on his seat. Heartfelt talk was a foreign language to him. And one of the many reasons he'd lost Sophia the first time. He needed to learn to open up about his feelings—if only it wasn't so hard.

"Will you help me?" he asked, desperation adding an edge to his voice.

She hesitated, her loyalties clearly torn between the three children. Finally, she gave a decisive nod. "*Sí*, I will help."

Tony sighed his relief. Now they just needed to come up with a foolproof plan.

16

Sophia took her time getting ready for dinner. Her childhood bedroom looked much the same as she'd left it, pink and girly. Matt had decorated it after his first big poker championship. She'd loved the delicate white princess bed—complete with canopy—downy pink comforter, and frilly pillows. She didn't have the heart to tell him she wasn't twelve anymore, and anyway, it was her sanctuary. The one place she could be herself—no expectations.

She ignored the hollow ache and indulged in a long soak in the Jacuzzi spa tub. The jets relieved some of the stress and she climbed out half an hour later refreshed. Her walk-in closet looked somewhat bare, with most of her clothes in New York, but she found a pair of blue jeans on the shelf and only had to suck in her tummy a little to get them done up. A butter-soft cornflower blue chambray shirt teamed up with the lapis lazuli earrings *Tía* Consuela had given her for her eighteenth birthday finished the outfit. She brushed her long hair until it shone and contemplated herself in the mirror. Her city clothes were stylish and gave her the confidence needed to face office politics, but they didn't compare to what she wore now. It was almost like she was two different people, the businesswoman chasing a corner office, and the country girl searching for a way to make a difference in her world. The big question was, which one suited her the most?

She turned her head at the muffled sound of a baby's cry. Poor Pippa. Consuela assured them her rosy red cheeks and temperature spikes meant she would soon get her first tooth. Sophia didn't know who hurt the most, her tiny niece, or Pippa's helpless father. Matt had been wandering around the past few days like a bear with its foot caught in a trap. Although, that could be due to the impending visit tonight from Aaron's big-time investor. So, yeah, she was dressing for success. If a showdown was going to happen, she needed to face it head on.

Satisfied with her pep-talk, she chose a bright shade of pink for her lips and used a tissue to blot the excess. Pumpkin wound around her ankles as though offering comfort and support.

"Come here, sweetheart." She picked the cat up

and nuzzled her furry neck. "Are you momma's baby kitty? Yes, you are." The answering soft rumble warmed Sophia's heart. She'd always felt a deep connection with her four-legged friends. At least with them, she could be herself. "I have to go make nice with the adults. If you're good, I'll bring you back a treat, okay?"

She carried Pumpkin to the bed and set her down, grimacing when the cat immediately started kneading the coverlet. "Do you have to?" She'd destroyed a leather sofa at home, but Sophia didn't have the heart to have her declawed. They'd compromised, Pumpkin could have the couch as long as she left the rest of the furniture alone.

Sighing, she slipped on a pair of open-toed heels, the same pink as her lips, and opened the door just as Tony raised his hand to knock on it from the other side. She stared at him for a surprised second before finding her voice. "H... hi. What are you doing here?"

Her pulse spiked. They hadn't talked since the confrontation at the graveyard. She couldn't believe she'd said those things. She wouldn't blame him if he ran in the other direction. No guy liked to have a woman confess her undying adoration for him out of the blue like that. What had she been thinking?

"Consuela asked me to walk you to dinner," he said, his gaze on her lips.

Well, that answered her question. He was there because he'd been asked, not to suddenly declare himself madly in love with her. She should know real life didn't work like it did in the fairytales.

"I'm pretty sure I know my way," she said, and yeah, it came out a trifle snarky. What did he expect? She didn't like feeling awkward in her own skin, but thanks to her runaway tongue her childhood love now knew she'd never gotten over him. Embarrassing? Hell, yeah. Annoying, too.

His gaze moved to her eyes and something like regret passed between them. "I wanted to check on you—make sure you're okay."

Sophia squared her shoulders. "Why wouldn't I be? My brothers hate each other, our home might be sold to the highest bidder, and you... well, anyway, I'm just hunkie-dory."

She moved to breeze past him, nose in the air, but he grasped her arm and swung her around to face him.

"You never let me finish the other day." He bent so he could see into her eyes. "I missed you, Sophia. I almost went after you so many times, but..." She tried to jerk away, and he tightened his hold. "*But*, I didn't want to hold you back. It was important for you to experience something other than ranch-life. To date— though it tore me apart to think of you with another man. You would have withered here, Soph, admit it—at least to yourself."

She glared at him, angrier than she could remember being in a very long time. Even her ears felt fiery. "Let me get this straight, you cared so much for me, you let me *leave*? For five damn years?" She shook her head and blinked the hot tears away. "How noble. Tony Morrison, always honorable, right? How does it feel to live up there in that exalted air? Lonely? 'Cause that's how I felt. Deserted. Sure, it was my decision to go, but I guess I thought someone—you—would care enough to at least call and check up on me. But you never did, did you?"

She gulped fresh air into burning lungs. This was too hard. She'd thought time had healed the hurt, but it had obviously burrowed itself deep inside and festered. Coming home was a mistake. She'd get through this meeting tonight, for Aaron's sake, and then make plans tomorrow to head back to New York. It was for the best.

Tony stared down into Sophia's averted face and wondered where he'd gone wrong. One minute he'd been trying to confess his feelings, and the next she'd attacked him like a fishwife. She was the one who left, dammit. True, he'd done nothing to stop her, but then, telling Sophia *not* to do something was like telling a tornado to disappear. She was a force of nature. He loved that about her even as it drove him crazy.

Her laugh was brittle. "This isn't getting us anywhere. I think we've said all there is to say—" He frowned at the finality in her voice, "—and frankly, it doesn't matter anymore. I've moved on, and I imagine you have, too."

He scowled, his chest tight. "What about all those things you said at the graveyard? The way you kissed me? None of that was real?"

Why did he always end up tied in knots around her? She frustrated him almost as much as she moved him. Being around Sophia Shaughnessy was like living in the center of a vortex, chaotic and calm at the same time. But he couldn't imagine his life without her.

She lifted her chin, those soft pink lips pursed in annoyance. "Of course, it was real. I was caught up in the moment. We have a history. It's not something I'd forget."

Really? He thought she'd done a damn fine job of doing just that. "I call bullshit," he snarled, suddenly fed up with her, them, everything. "You've done nothing but try to drive me crazy since the day I met you. Even as a teenager you'd pull stunts, so I'd take notice. Your daddy used to watch me like a hawk. I had to keep telling myself there was ten years between us. You were too young to know your own mind. It didn't matter though, I wanted you." He hauled her up against his chest, relishing the sound of her startled gasp. "And you wanted me, didn't you?" He gave her a little shake. *"Didn't you?"*

She nodded, her eyes wide. Satisfaction flared. Enough with all this evasion. They'd always done their best communication by touch. He swooped in and laid claim to her mouth, desire pounding like a sledge-hammer in his chest. She tasted like heaven and his own personal hell and he couldn't get enough. His tongue teased the lush fullness of her bottom lip. She sucked in a breath, and he smiled against her mouth. Then she licked her lips, soft tongue clashing with his. His knees buckled.

She moaned and lifted her arms to circle his neck as though she needed his help to stay upright, her fingers curling into the hair at his nape. The rasp of her nails on his skin sent shudders down his spine all the way to his butt. He pushed her back against the wall, his leg nudging her thighs apart, his hands luxuriating in the shape and feel of her waist, ribs, breasts. God, it had been too long. He lifted her leg and wrapped it around his hip, rocking his erection against her pelvis. His eyes crossed, it felt so damn good. Her nipples were puckered, inviting him to suckle. She rotated her hips, striking up an invitation he was powerless to resist.

"Take me to your bed," he whispered next to her ear.

She shivered in reaction, her eyes glazed as they stared into his. But then they began to clear, and he knew before she even said a word that the evening wasn't going to end the way he wanted.

She dropped her leg from his waist and stared a hole in his chest. "This isn't the answer, Tony. Let me go."

No, his heart cried, even as he released her and took a step back. "Sure, Princess. Whatever you say." Was that really him with the sarcastic don't-give-a-shit attitude?

Apparently, it was.

She looked up at him with wounded eyes before stepping into her room and gently closing the door in his face.

Tony clasped a hand to his chest, faintly surprised his heart hadn't quit beating. For one brief, shining moment they'd connected and he'd had a glimpse of a future he'd only dreamed about. One with Sophia as his wife, creating a life together. Then he'd opened his stupid mouth and it all came crashing around his feet.

He looked down, half-expecting to see pieces of his shattered heart spread upon the cool terracotta tiles.

Instead, he met the solemn gaze of Sophia's cat, Pumpkin. She must have escaped the room while they were...

He bent down and picked the fur-ball up. "What are you doing out here, huh? Your mistress will be worried." He lifted his hand to knock on her door, then hesitated when he heard a faint sobbing from the other side. Damn. He hadn't meant to make her cry. Should he knock anyway? *No, give her some privacy.*

He gave the cat an awkward pat. "You better come with me. We'll let her know where you are later." *When I figure out how to apologize.*

He cuddled Sophia's cat against his chest and strode down the hall, finding an odd comfort in the feline's purring body.

*a*aron was in the den pouring himself a stiff cocktail when Tony caught up to him. He turned and raised his glass in a toast. "Hey, buddy. Want a drink?"

He already had a good glow happening, going by the ruddy cheeks and glassy eyes. Tony nodded. "I'll take a beer. Should you be into the hard stuff before your big dinner meeting?"

Aaron twisted the cap off the bottle and passed it over, a sloppy grin on his face. "I'm celebrating. Big brother listened instead of acting like his word was final. I'm impressed," he said, enunciating each vowel with careful precision. "Maybe Sophia talked some sense into him after all."

Tony froze, the bottle halfway to his lips. Lips still sensitive from attempting to force his will onto this man's sister. He probably should keep that to himself. "Matt's fair. He wants the same thing all of you want. A legacy for your kids." He eyed the amber liquid cradled in Aaron's hands. "Not that you'll have to worry about that, you keep drinking the way you have been lately."

Aaron smirked, too far gone to take offence. "Don't worry, my boys know how to swim. I think the bigger question is, when do you plan on making an honest woman out of my sister?"

Shit, were they seen earlier?

No, Aaron was much too relaxed for a guy intent on defending his sister's honor. Tony took a long swig of his beer and tried to come up with an answer that didn't sound desperate. "You know Sophia, the more you want her to do one thing, the faster she goes in another direction." They both had a good laugh over that one, but it was true. She was as obstinate as the day was long.

"She's a handful, that's for sure. Our father encouraged her to be independent and always stand up for what she believed in." Aaron swallowed the last of his drink, set the glass on the bar, and wandered across the room to stare up at his grandparents' wedding picture over the stone fireplace's hand-hewn wooden mantle. "She looks like Grandma Maddie."

"Yes." It was in their strong chins and potency of

their expressions—able to draw attention with little more than a blink of long, dark lashes. "Beautiful women."

It was more than just their physical features, though they had a classic beauty that would carry them well throughout their lives. Maddison had been well known for her kind and generous heart. She'd often helped individuals in need, donating time and energy to make lives better for those less fortunate. Sophia carried the same trait, though her focus was abused animals. It broke her heart to see a creature in pain. She'd regularly brought strays home to nurse back to health, including Matt's hairless mutt, Chewy.

"Do you think she's happy?" Aaron had moved on to a framed photo of the three Shaughnessy siblings resting on an ebony baby grand piano sitting kitty-corner in the room.

Tony didn't need to see the picture to know what Aaron was looking at, the kids running through a field of bluebonnets in Hidden Valley, the old farmhouse in the background. The photo had been taken by their father on one of the last days they'd shared before the plane crash. Sophia was chasing her brothers and had glanced over her shoulder, face alight with laughter.

"Your sister?" he asked. "Hard to say. She holds her cards close to her chest, but yeah, I think she's doing okay." Even without him in the picture.

Aaron nodded and rubbed his jaw. "I hope you're right. She was the closest to our father, and then when Grandma Maddie went... she hasn't had an easy go of it."

None of them had. They were a close family—he'd envied that connection for a long time. His own clan would as soon spit in your eye as help each other. He cleared his throat. Maybe, now Aaron would be open to listening.

He joined his friend by the piano. "I wanted to talk to you about that—before tonight's shindig."

Aaron smirked and sat down to plunk out a few surprisingly melodious notes on the ivory keys. "Don't worry, buddy. I'll still drink with you when I'm rich and famous."

The drinking issue was a whole other conversation, Tony decided to save that one for another day. "You're going about this sale the wrong way."

Aaron hit a discordant note and dropped the lid on the piano. He rose and ignored Tony to wander over to the bar and pour himself another shot of whiskey. He took a healthy swallow—and barely winced as the straight alcohol slid down his throat—before answering. "It ain't really any of your business, is it?"

So much for the soft approach.

"No, it's not. But I *do* have a vested interest in

Sophia. You selling this ranch out from under her feet isn't right, and you know it."

Aaron gave him the squint-eye. "She put you up to this?"

Tony clucked his tongue, disgusted. "Do you even know your sister? If she has something to say, she says it. She sure as hell wouldn't send me to do her talking for her." He shook his head. "This is between you and me. I've worked this land for close to twenty years now, ever since your dad took me in and gave me a chance. I've seen this family stumble, and even fall a couple of times, but you've always picked yourselves up and been better for it. You know why?" He pointed at Aaron's chest. "Because you stuck together. I don't know what's going on, but it's not too late to straighten this out." He'd be lucky if he wasn't out of a job after this. "C'mon, man, be the hero your dad would want you to be, stop this sale—at least for now—talk to your brother and sister, find a solution you all agree on." *Before it's too late.*

Aaron's skin took on a green cast. He stared at the drink in his hand as though he didn't know how it got there, then looked up and met Tony's gaze.

His heart dropped into his stomach. "What did you do?"

"It's too late. I signed the papers yesterday."

18

*A*ndy Sylvester was younger than Sophia expected, but carried the confidence and charm of a man used to getting his way.

Too bad that wasn't going to happen today.

"How is it you know my brother, Aaron, Mr. Sylvester?" Aaron was a farm boy through and through. He left the ranch long enough to blow off steam in Houston or one of the smaller towns nearby, and then he came home. She couldn't see these two together, it made no sense. Unless...

"He dated my sister, Trish. She introduced us." Andy's smile and his blue eyes coaxed her to relax, seeming to suggest he was harmless. She knew better.

"Trish, huh?" She turned to her brother who sat moping at the other end of the dinner table. "You didn't tell me you had a girlfriend." She didn't know who made the seating arrangements, but she was grateful. Aaron was better off far away from this shark.

A dark red flush stained his cheeks and his gaze skittered away. "She's not my girlfriend. We went out a few times, that's all. Don't you-all have better things to talk about than my non-existent love life?" He played with the mashed potatoes on his plate, then dropped the fork and reached for the ever-present whiskey glass near his elbow.

Matt wiped his mouth with a napkin, set it carefully on the table next to his plate, and sent a wry smile to their guest. "Ignore my brother, his manners seem to have disappeared with the liquor in his glass." Aaron snorted around the mouth of the tumbler.

Andy waved an expansive hand. "It's no trouble, Trish wasn't really his type. I'm just glad it didn't hamper our business dealings."

Tony had joined the family for dinner and frowned. "Does she know where your loyalties lie?"

Sophia hid her smile behind her hand. Andy wasn't gaining many admirers with his attitude.

"Hey, you can't judge a guy for trying to make a buck. Right, Aaron?" Andy met Tony's glare and offered him a basket of fresh-baked buns. "You might not understand, seeing as you're a laborer, but we have a vision. With a little capital investment this ranch could become the next Piney Point or River Oaks," he said enthusiastically, naming the ritziest neighborhoods in Houston.

Tony helped himself to a dinner roll, ignoring the proffered basket. He used his knife to slice the top off the bun and lathered the insides with butter before handing it to Sophia.

"Well, this *employee* still knows how to treat a woman with respect. Your sister is sweet and doesn't deserve your rude remarks."

Sophia halted, the warm bun halfway to her lips, and stared at Tony. What did he mean, *she was sweet*? It sounded like he knew the missing Trish and cared about her. The bread lost its appeal. She set it on the side of her plate and wiped her fingertips on a napkin. What did she expect? It had been five years, Tony was bound to have dated. Heck, so had she—lots. Okay, some. She'd dated sporadically, preferring to focus on her career. There were even a couple of really nice guys, but none made her heart quiver or her temper soar. That honor went to Anthony Morrison, damn him.

Matt broke into the conversation. "Sorry you wasted your time, but this ranch will never become a hideaway for the rich and famous." He leaned forward, his eyes hard. "My—our—great-grandfather founded this homestead with the intention of passing it on to his children and their kids and so on for generations to come. I'll be damned if I'll allow it to go to the highest bidder."

Cassandra placed her hand on his clenched fist resting on the table and Matt slowly relaxed into his chair. "Whatever Aaron's told you, forget it. This land is not for sale—now, or ever."

The room went still other than the ticking of Grandma Maddie's cuckoo clock hanging on the wall. His face a sullen mask, Aaron started clapping.

"That's some speech, brother. You should run for governor, you'd be a shoe-in."

"Aaron," Sophia warned. "You're not helping your cause."

He snorted. "It doesn't matter what I say, Matt's made up his mind." He sent her an almost apologetic glance before leveling a stubborn gaze on his brother. "Too bad you have no say. We each received a section of land in the will, I can do what I want with my piece —and that includes selling it so I can donate my share to the main ranch."

Matt swore. "Why can't you trust me to make things right?" He shoved his chair back and stood, drawing a startled gasp from Cassandra. "I bet Grandma Maddie is rolling over in her grave." He stomped out the door without another word, leaving an uncomfortable silence in his wake.

Cassandra gave an uncertain smile and set the

napkin in her lap onto her unfinished plate. "I better go —he might need me." She rose and hurried after Matt.

Andy coughed and reached for his glass of water. "Family theatrics, gotta love 'em, right?"

Tony looked disgusted. "This ain't no circus, man. You're screwing with people's feelings here. Just because it means nothing to you, have some decency." He reached over and grasped Sophia's hand, his grip warm and comforting.

She drew strength from his touch and tried to find the right words to defuse an explosive situation. "Matt appreciates you making such a big sacrifice, Aaron." He glared past her to the doorway his brother had stormed through. "Really, he does. But, did you consider how guilty you were going to make him feel?"

Aaron turned misery-filled eyes in her direction. "I thought it was the right thing to do. Christ, sis, he gave up hundreds of thousands of dollars to keep this ranch viable. Why is it wrong for me to do the same?"

Her heart ached for her brothers. They were so stubborn. If she could just get them to sit down and hash it out... She was hit by a suddenly brilliant idea.

"Let's have a picnic."

Tony's jaw dropped, and Aaron stared at her like she'd lost her mind. Andy grinned and nodded, no doubt thinking it would be in his honor.

"Have you gone loco?" Aaron asked.

"Maybe," she agreed. "But it's been a long time since I've been to the cabin, and I want to go. Besides, it's Matt and Cassandra's anniversary next week. It would be perfect timing." She squeezed Tony's hand. "It might be our last chance." Especially since her great-grandfather's old cabin sat on Aaron's chunk of land.

Tony waited for everyone to leave the room except Aaron. He rose and shut the dining room doors, his anger tightly controlled. Sophia seemed barely able to hold back tears as she bid them goodnight—all except for that scumbag, Andy Sylvester. She'd steered clear of him, thank God.

He leaned against the wall and watched his friend stare at nothing. It sucked when no one appreciated your sacrifices, he should know.

"They'll come around," he offered. "It was a shock, that's all."

Aaron shook his head, the blond curls glinting under the chandelier. "Thanks, but I doubt it. Matt looked like he wanted to rip my head off my shoulders, and Sophia... I just wanted to help."

Tony took a chair next to him, not sure what to say. "Are you positive you want to go through with the sale?"

Aaron looked at him with bloodshot eyes. "I told you, I signed the papers. There ain't no backing out now."

Tony nodded and leaned back in his seat, his hand playing with a spoon on the table. "What if I was to tell you that you can get out of selling? You might need to pay restitution, along with any deposits he's given you, but it can be done."

Aaron sat up, hope chasing the clouds from his expression. "Are you sure? How do you know?"

Tony swallowed the ball in his throat. "My folks are big-time lawyers. I contacted them to ask." And wasn't *that* a lovely conversation.

Aaron blinked tear-wet eyes and reached over to give him a rough man-hug. Drunk or not, it warmed Tony's heart.

"Thanks, man. I don't know what to say."

Tony's smile was lopsided, but he didn't think it was noticed. "Don't worry about it, they're happy to help." Or at least, happy to have their long-lost son under their domineering thumbs again.

19

S ophia spent the next couple of days avoiding Tony. She felt vulnerable after the dinner fiasco and needed time to figure out what to do next, so she dove into the picnic plans as though something as simple as food and flowers could save the ranch. Or her fractured family.

Today she'd decided to ride out to Hidden Valley and see how much sprucing up the old cabin needed before the picnic. She wasn't planning anything as elaborate as they had done for Matt and Cassandra's wedding, but she still wanted to spiff the place up— and remind Aaron of his roots.

"Good morning, Cleopatra." She greeted her horse as she entered the barn stall. "How's my girl today?" The Appaloosa tossed her head, the black mane rippling on her silky neck. "Ready to get out of here?"

Cleo nickered. Sophia smiled and reached for the bridle hanging outside the pen.

"Where are we going?"

Tony's breath tickled the back of her fingers, sending shivers up her arm. She gasped and yanked her hand back. "You scared the heck out of me. What are you doing sneaking up on people that way?"

He opened the bottom of the Dutch-door and entered the stall, bridle in hand and blue eyes warm with laughter. "Your horse knew I was here," he said. He gave Cleo a welcoming rub between the ears and slid the bridle on at the same time. "Going for a ride?"

She tore her gaze away from the muscles of his back and gulped. "I... thought I'd take a trip out to Hidden Valley, check on the cabin."

He nodded. "Okay, give me a minute to saddle up and I'll keep you company."

Her heart fluttered. There was no denying it, the thought of spending a day with Tony away from the curious eyes of her family created butterflies in her stomach. "Do you think that's a good idea?"

Tony tipped her chin up and bestowed a light peck on her mouth that turned into something more—something she never wanted to end. When he lifted his head, their lips clung as though knowing they belonged together. "Are you saying you don't want me to come, sweetheart?"

No. Yes. I don't know.

"Well, hurry up if you're coming, I don't have all day," she said, self-defense making her irritable.

He grinned and tipped his worn cowboy hat over his brow. "Yes, ma'am."

She followed his very fine butt out of the stall and led Cleo to the tack room. Tony met her there a moment later, his bay trailing behind him like a placid dog.

"Here, let me get that." He brushed by her—leaving the fresh scent of hay, pine and cinnamon in his wake—and lifted the leather saddle off the stand as though it weighed nothing.

She hurried to grab the wool pads and spread them across the horses' broad backs, then stood out of the way so Tony could fling the saddles into place. A few minutes later they were cinched, and he turned to offer her a hand up.

"I can do it." She laughed. "I haven't been in New York *that* long." Though the thought of his hands around her waist tempted her to pretend otherwise.

He stepped back, hands in the air and a smile on those kissable lips. "Prove it, city girl," he teased, hat pushed back on his head and coffee-colored curls peeking from under the brim.

Cleo nodded as though in agreement, her bridle jingling.

When did her horse get so tall?

She caught the pommel with her left hand and used her right to hold the stirrup in place while trying to get her left toe into the loop. What once was accomplished with one fluid motion now became more of a comedic act. Cleopatra sidestepped, forcing Sophia to hop in order to retain her balance. In the next moment a warm palm planted itself on her butt, gave a push, and she was up and landed in the saddle with a soft *ooph*.

Tony—smart man—refrained from saying anything, though his laughing eyes spoke volumes. He handed her the reins and turned away to climb into his saddle with an economy of movement. The show-off.

"You sure you want to ride all the way to the cabin?" he asked. "It's a two-hour trip there and back, and you're kind of out of practice."

She stiffened and gathered up the reins. "Are you forgetting I was once the barrel racing champion in these parts, Tony Morrison?"

He grinned and doffed his hat once more. "My mistake. Lead the way, but don't blame me if you can't walk for a week after we get back home."

Huh. She'd show him.

She cleared the barn and the courtyard, then signaled her horse by clenching her knees. "Let's go, girl."

Cleo let out a joyful neigh and took off over the open ground at a fast clip, happy to be given her head. Sophia laughed too, feeling the weight of the past few days dissipate under the warm blue sky of a perfect June day. They frightened the odd rabbit into hopping away, and once, in the distance, a small herd of deer looked up from grazing at the sound of their passing before taking flight, the white plumes on their tails waving like banners. They rode through a new crop of hay, the stalks so high it brushed the horses' underbellies. Birds sang and flitted here and there, gathering nest material and feeding on the bugs eating the hay. The cycle of life. It was comforting to know they were all a part of God's plan. Her parents and grandparents may have left this earth, but the land they had sown still produced and nourished the Shaughnessy heirs.

For now, anyway.

Tony let her take the lead for the first mile or two, then caught up and kept pace beside her, their knees occasionally bumping with the horse's strides. He could ride like this forever and be a happy man. She appeared more relaxed than he'd seen in a very long time. He hated to bring up the ranch business but needed her to know about Aaron's change of heart. It hurt to see the friction between a normally close family —unlike his own.

"Crops are looking good," he said by way of an opener, then cursed under his breath. Way to prove he was little more than a country hick. He reached into the saddlebag and withdrew a metal flask filled with strong, black coffee. "Thirsty?" He offered her the steel carafe.

She raised an eyebrow. "Kind of early for drinking, isn't it?"

He frowned. "I don't drink on the job. It's coffee. I made it before heading out to the barn this morning."

It was her turn to scowl. "So that's what I am, a job?" She gave her horse a little nudge with her heel and surged ahead. "I don't need you to babysit me. Go do whatever it is you're supposed to be doing." *And leave me alone*, was more than apparent in the set of her shoulders.

Tony sighed. There was no figuring women out. He hurried to catch up and reached over to grab her reins, slowing Cleopatra to a halt. "Hold on a minute. I never said anything about you being a *job*. Truth is, I should be riding fence today, but when I saw you heading out I changed my plans. You've saved me from a long, hard ride and I wanted to show my appreciation by sharing my *delicious* coffee with you, but forget it. All the more for me."

He unscrewed the flask, inhaled the robust flavor, then took a long drink before replacing the lid and turning to lift the flap on his saddlebag. A hand on his arm stopped his movement. One glance into Sophia's contrite eyes and he felt himself slipping into those golden-brown depths.

"I'm sorry, Tony. I always seem to overreact around you." She held her hand out for the coffee flask. "Can I have a do-over?"

He smiled, relieved he'd averted her suspicions. Truth was Matt had asked him to keep an eye on her after the episode with the rogue stallion. Not that he needed to, there was no way Tony was taking any chances with Sophia's safety.

The smooth line of her throat was exposed as she tipped her head to receive the drink and his chest grew warm. She stole his breath. If only he wasn't so old and jaded maybe they could have stood a chance. If she'd have anything to do with him after today's confession.

Needing to escape his demons he tempted her with the one thing he knew she couldn't refuse. "Let's race!"

20

The cabin crouched at the far end of Hidden Valley—so named due to the secret entrance through a rocky crevice. Sophia's great-grandfather happened upon it while searching the brush for calves and immediately fell in love with the beautiful hideaway.

There were so many precious family memories associated with this valley; her father holding her hand as the boys cavorted in the deep grass, her grandfather's pride in the furniture he'd fashioned for the small, one room bungalow, swinging from the branches of a giant cottonwood that bordered the lazy creek and meandered through the bottom end of the field. The roof had been falling in five years ago when she'd ridden here with Tony in search of her missing brother, Matt, and his fiancée, Cassandra. It was only later that the family found the engagement was a hoax to ease their dying grandmother's heart. Except the joke was on Matt, he fell in love and didn't realize it until he almost lost the girl. But the magic of this valley had done its job, they'd reconnected, admitted their feelings, and were married on a gorgeous June day like this one—right here at the cabin.

Sophia studied the way Tony rode his horse, and the relaxed curve of his spine as he let the bay pick its way down the gentle slope. The width of his shoulders was outlined by a pale blue chambray shirt and muscular jean-clad thighs hugged his horse's girth. He was one fine looking man. She'd crushed on him as a teen and it never faded, unlike many first loves. Where most of her friends had moved on and created new relationships—marriages and children—she never had. Only now, riding into this enchanted valley, could she admit she wanted the fairytale. Except, in her case the prince slept and she needed to bestow true love's kiss.

"What's with the secretive smile?" he asked, glancing back and catching her daydreaming.

Good thing the sun was packing some heat and could be used to explain her blush. She spread her arm to encompass the view. "I was remembering all the times I used to pretend I was a princess when my dad brought us here. My brothers were knights sent to destroy the dragon and save the kingdom." She grinned. "Kids have the best imaginations."

Instead of the expected smile, Tony's expression turned grim.

"What is it? Did I say something wrong?" she asked, spurring her horse closer.

He shook his head, but she could see he was disturbed. "Nah, it's nothing. Let's get down there and see if the old place is still standing."

She shivered as a chill breeze suddenly kicked up and ruffled her hair. Some of the joy leached out of the day. The easy camaraderie they'd shared was gone and the rest of the journey was accomplished in silence.

The log cabin looked better than Sophia expected. The porch had a fresh coat of gleaming white paint, windows sparkled, and the old, warped door had been replaced with a sturdier version. "Someone's been busy," she murmured.

"I enjoyed it," Tony said, slipping out of the saddle and wrapping reins around the porch rail. "Matt asked me if I wanted to stay here when I needed some down-time and I jumped on it. Thought the least I could do was fix it up."

He moved to her side and lifted his hands. "Here, I'll help you down."

Her heart somersaulted. She was going to land in his arms, there was no avoiding it. She took a steadying breath and swung her leg over Cleopatra's neck, then slid down, using Tony's shoulders for support. She stumbled a little on the landing and gasped, but he had her. His hands on her waist held her upright and close... so close, to his chest.

"Thank you," she mumbled, flustered. The latent strength in those arms invited her touch. He was nearing forty, a man in his prime, and everything inside her stilled, aware of him as never before. "I'm such a klutz." She laughed, trying to lighten the mushrooming tension. Between the heat of the horse at her back and the intensity of the man holding her captive, she was on fire.

In danger of combustion.

"Sophia," he said. "Look at me."

In that moment, she was helpless to do anything other than what he demanded. Her gaze climbed the rock wall of his chest, lingered on the betraying flicker of pulse that showed in the taut line of his throat, hesitated on lips with the power to bring pleasure or pain, and meshed with eyes the turbulent color of a gas flame.

"What are we doing, Tony?" The question was innocuous, but contained a wealth of emotion. This push-pull game they'd played for years was wearing her down. Either he admitted his feelings right now, in this instant, or she was done.

Typical Tony, he took a step back, his face closing as though to re-erect the wall he'd built around himself, but not today. She wasn't letting him.

"Tell me about your childhood," she implored, placing her palm over his heart. "I was thinking about mine on the way here and realized I know nothing about your past. Do you have brothers or sisters? Are your parents alive? Where did you grow up? What was it like?"

He covered her hand with his and the warmth seeped up her arm and set hope to fluttering in her chest.

"You're right, I guess it's time." He tugged her toward the stairs. "Let's sit on the swing and I'll explain."

Curious, and concerned, Sophia followed him to the wooden swing hanging from the rafters. Her grandfather had made the beautiful piece for Grandma Maddie so she could sit and watch the sunsets with him.

She waited until she and Tony were settled before she said more. "Look, if you're not comfortable talking..."

He laced their fingers together and gazed into her eyes. "Why are you always so nice to me? If I were you I'd be demanding to know who I had working for me."

She frowned and tried unsuccessfully to pull her

hand free. "You think this is about your *job*? I think we both know it's more than that. I care about you, Tony. I want to learn who you are, what makes you tick. Is that so wrong?"

He gave her a too-short kiss. "Of course not. I... care about you, too." He wrapped an arm around her waist and leaned back, forcing her to follow suit or fall into his lap. "Just give me a minute to get my thoughts in order, okay?"

She reluctantly nodded and relaxed against his side. It really was beautiful. The wind soughed through the trees bordering the field and made waves in the tall grasses. Bluebonnets and Indian Paintbrush poked their heads up along the bank of the creek, creating vibrant splashes of color while the sun played peekaboo with cumulus clouds overhead. If she tried hard enough she could almost believe they were a newly married couple in love and the cabin was their honeymoon getaway.

Almost.

"I had a brother. Leo died a long time ago. I killed him."

The words dumped ice on her fantasies. It was as though the pretty blue-sky day turned cold and gray. Then she processed what he had said and rejected it out of hand. She turned her head on his shoulder and looked up at the grim face of the man she would trust with her life.

"What happened? Because there's no way I'm going to believe you deliberately hurt your brother," she said, lifting a hand to his tensed jaw. "That's not who you are."

He frowned, then gusted out a heavy sigh and kissed her palm before lowering her hand to his thigh. "I wish I had your faith." He stared across the field, his expression faraway. "I was ten, Leo seven. My parents had this big function to go to but our normal sitter backed out at the last minute. They were upset—it was an important gathering—and I wanted to help so I said I could watch him. We'd catch some TV, then go to bed early, no problem. Except, Leo choked on a kernel of popcorn and it wouldn't come out. I tried everything I'd seen them do on television, but nothing worked. His lips and the veins around his eyes turned blue and then he passed out." His eyes were full of past ghosts when he looked at her. "The emergency people took too long getting to our house, we lived on the outskirts of the city. Leo was dead before they arrived. I knew he was gone, but I couldn't let go of his hand. I... it felt wrong to let go."

His thigh was rock hard beneath her hand, the strain transmitting his pain. Sophia's chest hurt for the boy he'd been. Alone when he'd needed his parents the most.

"There was nothing you could do," she said, aching to heal the scars of the past. "It wasn't your fault."

A harsh sound exploded from his lips. He freed himself from her and rose, putting space between them physically and mentally. He paced from one end of the porch to the other, oblivious to the shying horses.

"Too bad my parents didn't feel the same way," he growled. "They sent me to a strict boarding school. Naturally, I revolted and ended up in a shitload of trouble." He slowed and looked at her again. "That's when I met your dad. I'd probably be dead or in jail by now if it wasn't for him. He gave me a chance when no one else would."

He sat beside her and took her hand. "Don't you see? I owed him my life. I vowed to make him proud. Somehow, I don't think screwing around with his daughter would've fit the bill."

Okay, she could see where he was coming from, but what they had together was more than '*screwing around*' as he put it.

"Tony, do you love me at all?" she asked, her heart in her throat.

"Of course. What's not to love?" He smiled, making light of her question.

She yanked her hand away. "I'm serious, you big

buffoon!" It was her turn to walk off her anxiety. "I've loved you ever since I can remember, Tony Morrison, but if you can't commit to me, or even say the words then I'm just going to... to scream."

She cringed. Very adult of her. So much for a civilized conversation. She always reverted to cavewoman around him. If only he wasn't so aggravating.

He slowly rose and came toward her, a beautiful animal stalking his prey. She backed up, suddenly nervous, until her butt hit the railing.

He boxed her in, hands on the rail by her hips, and leaned close to her ear. His breath sent goosebumps skating up and down her arms. "The only scream I want to hear from those pretty lips of yours is you crying my name when we make love." His teeth nibbled her lobe. "And believe me, I'm committed."

21

*S*he scared him, this warrior princess who seemed determined to drag his heart from his chest. Tony breathed in her scent, a flowery blend of everything he loved about summer, and cursed himself for an idiot. He'd admitted things to her today he hadn't shared with anyone—not even her father.

He'd carried the shame of letting his little brother die for so many years, yet somehow Sophia's questions had burrowed under his skin and freed the guilt demanding to be heard.

He was running scared now. Even as he rejoiced in the feel of her undeniable response to his touch, the taste of her on his lips, he was doing his damnedest to push her away.

"Ready to get this party started?" he whispered, and an insistent part of his body prayed she agreed.

"We should take this inside." He stepped back and held out his hand, the smallest bit of decency he had left insisting it be her choice.

She stared at him with eyes that saw too much. "I'll go with you," she agreed. "As soon as you quit blaming yourself."

Annoyance flashed. "Like you did with your family?" he growled. "Your whole life has been all about proving yourself to ghosts. Your parents are gone, they don't give a shit whether you build a guest ranch or a freaking zoo."

If he'd sucker-punched her it would have hurt less. Her face became ashen and tears turned her eyes to topaz gemstones. Frustrated or not, he had no business lashing out that way. He was a class-A asshole, no doubt about it.

"Honey, I'm sorry," he said, and reached to take her into his arms, but she leaned away, precariously close to going over the railing.

"Don't," she snapped. "You're finally speaking your mind. But, you're wrong. I *have* worked hard to become someone *I* could be proud of, not that I expect you to understand." She swiped angrily at the moisture on her cheeks and swung around to stare at the sun-dappled field. "See the grass out there? It's sweet and tender and nurtures all the wildlife in this valley, except for the wildflowers. The roots have to be strong to survive. The wildflowers have no choice, if they want to survive they must grip the steep banks of the stream. They have to hang on whether it's flooding or down to a near trickle because if they don't... they'll lose their place in the valley."

She turned to face him, her gaze resolute. "I'm just fighting for my place, Tony. I think I've earned that right."

He released a breath he hadn't realized he was holding. She was so freaking amazing. He'd never forgive himself if he hurt her the way his parents had hurt him. Trust was such a fragile gift. The wrong words could shatter it into a million irreconcilable pieces. He'd sooner cut out his own tongue than do that, yet he'd come close. Too close.

He offered the only thing he could—hope. "I never told you what my parents do for a living, did I? Why they had to attend that function the night my brother died, and so many like it?"

She shook her head and he could see the disappointment in her gaze. She thought he was changing the subject, ignoring what was essential to her. She couldn't be more wrong.

"They're corporate lawyers, important ones. I contacted them last week." His lips quirked at her start of surprise. "Yeah, I shocked them, too. Thing is, I knew if anyone could find a loophole to stop the sale of

Aaron's land, it was them." He took her hand and squeezed. "It worked, honey. Aaron's going to have to cough up some cash, but the land stays in the family. It's secured."

He didn't know what he expected, but it wasn't the tears.

"You... you did that, for us?" she cried. "Oh, Tony." She flung herself into his arms, her chest heaving with sobs. "After all these years. I can't believe you did that. Are you okay? What did th... they say?"

She was soaking his shirt, but he didn't care. He held on tight, his hand buried in her silky hair. "That's the funny part. Apparently, they'd hired an investigator years ago to track me down. They've known where I was the whole time." He didn't want to get into how that little tidbit made him feel. "Anyhow, now that I've reached out, they'd like to come out here—they're in Denver—maybe stay for a while. I told them I'd talk to the owner of the guest ranch, see if she had room." He smiled when she lifted her head, her nose pink from crying. "What do you think, boss-lady, ready for your first clients?"

She searched his eyes. "I can't believe your parents knew where you were and never tried to reach out to you. That's terrible."

Yeah, it kind of was. But, that was on them. He was done beating himself up about something he'd come to see he had no control over. He'd taken first aid and CPR training since then. If anything happened again, he'd be ready this time. His parents had gone through a nightmare as well. They'd blamed themselves for leaving him with Leo at such a tender age and it almost cost them their marriage. The cold silences and bitter words had driven him away. Where Sophia's family had bonded over their losses, his had fragmented.

It hadn't been easy making that call. His mother had answered the phone. She'd sounded older, tired.

"Hey, Mom. It's me, Anthony." They'd always called him by his formal name. It was solid, they said. It would help him grow up strong and firm.

The phone remained silent for so long he checked the connection.

"Anthony," she breathed. "I can't believe it's really you."

An unexpected lump formed in his throat. He'd been prepared for censure. He didn't know what to do with the remorse he heard in her voice.

"It's been a long time, Mom. How's Dad?" These two had once meant the world to him. He remembered a time, before Leo was gone, when they'd been happy. He suddenly ached to recapture that connection. To get his family back.

She gave a slightly giddy laugh. "He's fine. Wheeling and dealing, as usual. He'll be sorry he missed your call." She hesitated. "We both miss you, son."

Then why didn't you look for me? He wanted to cry. But that wasn't what he'd called for. "I need some advice for a friend," he said, his tone abrupt. Rehashing the past wouldn't accomplish anything. What was done, was done.

She cleared her throat. "I... I see. Of course. I'm happy to do what I can."

He blocked out the tears he heard and explained Aaron's situation. "What do you think? Can you help him?"

He listened as she clicked keys on the computer. "I just emailed your father. He's represented Sylvester Enterprises in the past, they owe him a favor. Send me the information and we'll see what we can do. The Shaughnessy Ranch is rich land, it would be a shame to see it turned into a housing community."

He nodded. "Yes." Then it dawned on him what she'd said. "How do you know about the ranch, Mom? I only just told you about it."

"I'm your mother, Anthony. Did you honestly believe I wouldn't find out where you were? If you were d... dead or alive?"

Stunned, he could only stand there and try to process this news. "Why didn't you call me then?"

"I wanted to," she said quietly. "I should have. I

don't have the right to ask, nevertheless I hope you'll forgive me."

His instinct shouted *no*, but his heart disagreed. He'd spent too many years without them in his life. It was time to mend some bridges. "There's nothing to forgive, Mom. Love you."

"Oh, son. We love you, too."

"Tony?"

Sophia's worried voice dragged him back to the present. He kissed her gently on the lips and tasted the tears she'd wept. This strong, independent woman humbled him with her compassionate soul. It showed itself in a multitude of ways, from the love she lavished on her baby niece, her brothers, her pets, and even a broken-down old cowboy like him.

"I was just thinking about all the time we've wasted." He smiled. "I know, that's your line. It's true, though. It's not that I don't care. I'd do anything for you. You've had me wrapped around this little finger —" he held up her index finger, "—since you were sweet sixteen."

She up and punched his arm.

"Ow! What'd you do that for?" Here he was confessing his feelings and she hit him. *Women.*

She glared. "We could have been married and had a passel of kids by now, that's why. You're so stubborn. I knew you cared. I just knew it."

"Yeah, well, you didn't have two burly men warning you to leave their baby sister alone or there'd be hell to pay." That was a bit of a stretch. They had warned him, but that wasn't the reason he'd backed off. He'd needed time to heal, and she'd needed to grow into the woman she'd become.

She gave a not-so-delicate snort. "Matt and Aaron think you're their brother-from-another mother. They'd be over the moon to see me settled."

"Are you asking me to marry you?" he teased.

Her eyes flashed. "And what if I am?" she said, not to be outdone.

The gravity of the moment took hold. Her cheeks flushed red, then turned pale, leaving two bright flags of color. She'd squared her shoulders, but he could almost hear her teeth chattering with nerves. He was the complete opposite. The moment the words came out, a sense of rightness filled his chest. This woman-child, whom he'd fallen for all those years ago, was finally going to be his wife.

He slowly dropped to one knee and took her hand in his. "I love you, Sophia Shaughnessy, and it would be my supreme honor if you would agree to take my hand in marriage forever more."

Her gaze was luminous. She took his face in trembling hands. "Yes. Yes. A thousand times, yes. I love you, Tony Morrison, now and forever." Her face crumpled, and her lips quivered as she leaned down to kiss him. "I should be mad you made me wait so long, but this made it all worthwhile."

He looked into her beautiful face and knew he'd come home.

EPILOGUE

ONE YEAR LATER

Sophia peeked out at the crowd gathering in front of her great-grandfather's cabin. Hundreds of miniature fairy lights twinkled from the branches of the giant cottonwood and the open-air gazebos set up along the bank of the babbling brook. They'd decided on a twilight wedding and caterers wandered among the guests offering flameless candles and yellow and white boxes with little metal handles. Each carton contained two butterflies, one for the bride and one for the groom, and would be released at the end of the ceremony. Chairs faced the porch of the cabin festooned in daisies and ribbons interwoven to match the butterfly boxes. Torches flickered, and country music played quietly in the background. It looked exactly as she'd imagined.

"Come away from there, child. I need to finish your

hair," *Tía* Consuela chided. "You don't want to be late to your own wedding, do you?"

Sophia smiled and put a hand to her fluttering tummy. "I'm a nervous wreck."

Consuela lifted Grandma Maddie's Spanish lace veil and set it gently over Sophia's upswept chignon. Tears glittered as they stared into the mirror.

"You look just like her, *pequeña*." Consuela dabbed at her eyes before fussing with the trailing ends of ivory lace. "Your grandmother would be so proud you chose to wear her gown."

Sophia brushed trembling fingers under her eyes. "Stop, you're going to make me cry." She'd have given anything to have her grandma with her today, but her spirit lived on within the threads of the gown and the location she'd chosen for the wedding.

The dress was exquisite. Matte organza with an overlay of floral appliques and strapless, it hugged her body to the waist, then flowed outward into a stunning train lined with sequins and seed pearls. She was a little taller than Maddie, but she'd used that to her advantage. She'd chosen to wear red leather cowboy boots beneath the dress. She hoped Tony would get the message she wanted to impart; *You could take the girl out of the country, but you couldn't take the country out of the girl.*

He'd been instrumental in saving the ranch and

helping her convince Matt and Aaron to give her business plan a chance. The hacienda had undergone a makeover, separating the family from their guests with common areas such as the kitchen and den. Though more household staff was needed to keep up with the cleaning requirements, Consuela enjoyed cooking authentic Tex-Mex food for their visitors. Matt took the guests on tours of his horse sheds, and Aaron did overnight camping on the range trips. There'd been some adjustments, but overall it was working out better than she'd expected. They were making money and the ranch stayed in Shaughnessy hands, win-win.

"Pippa, come here you little munchkin," Cassandra called from her seat at the makeup mirror.

Sophia scooped up the giggling baby just before she escaped the tent they'd set up for a change room. She looked adorable in a frothy white tutu, her curly blond hair bouncing with every uneven step. "Wait for us, missy," she said, tickling the chubby belly. Pippa had started walking a month ago and was a going concern. She kept her parents on their feet.

"She will be so cute leading the wedding march," Consuela murmured.

It was important to Sophia that everyone she loved be a part of her day. With that thought in mind, she turned to the elderly woman. "I know it's last minute, but I wanted it to be a surprise," she said. "Will you walk me down the aisle?"

Consuela's jaw dropped. "Me?" She started laughing and crying at the same time. "*Sí, sí.* It would be my honor."

Pippa stared at her wide-eyed, no doubt surprised to see all these adults bawling like babies. "Mama," she cried, pudgy limbs stretching out for her mother. "Mama, hold."

Sophia set her down before the waterworks began and she plunged across the room into her mother's waiting arms.

The music changed, and the opening chords of the wedding march rang out across the valley. Sophia's heart jumped.

It was time.

"Are you ready, *pequeña*?" Consuela's smile was watery.

The nerves settled. She was about to marry the love of her life. She was more than ready, she was eager. "Let's do this."

Cassandra went first in a pale yellow form-fitting sheath that looked stunning on her curvy figure. Pippa trailed after her mother, tossing rose petals out of a white wicker basket whenever she thought of it. The crowd oohed and aahed and Matt's smile was incandescent.

Sophia took in Aaron's western suit and tie, before she found her husband-to-be. Tony stood slightly apart from the other men in a classic dark suit teamed with a white dress shirt and a boutonnière made up of a single yellow rose and sprigs of baby's breath.

He stole her breath away.

"Here we go," Consuela whispered.

The guests rose as she and Consuela began their journey and the nerves she'd thought under control fluttered to life, an entire carnival in her chest. Tony's parents stood in the front row, their expressions filled with love and affection. The Morrisons had spent a lot of time on the ranch over the past year and Sophia was thrilled the relationship with their son was improving. She looked at her brothers. Family ties, they meant the world to her.

Mrs. Morrison, Peggy, grasped her hand and kissed her cheek. "Make him happy," she whispered. "He deserves it."

Sophia's smile wobbled. More than anything she ached to create an incredible life with Anthony Morrison. She nodded. "Yes, ma'am. I plan to."

Then they were at the foot of the stairs and Tony was there to take her hand. He stared into her eyes with such love and promise, her heart overflowed.

"I love you," he murmured. "Ready to make it official?"

She smiled around her tears. "About time."

As they climbed the steps up to the porch a shrill call resounded across the valley. Tony pointed toward the hill Sophia had stood on with her father all those years ago. The rogue stallion stared at the humans invading his domain, his white coat reflecting the rays from a setting sun.

"It's him," she whispered. "Do you think he's here to give us his blessing?"

Tony hugged her close and kissed her forehead. "Maybe your dad and my brother sent him."

The horse trumpeted once more, then wheeled and disappeared from view, leaving a reverent silence in his wake.

Yeah, she liked that thought.

PREVIEW HOLD 'EM

GAMBLING HEARTS #1

Cassandra barely waited until they had left Matt's

family behind for the cool, terracotta comfort of the house before she turned on him.

"I am *not* sleeping with you," she hissed, all but stamping her foot. Lapis-lazuli eyes snapped like fireflies and her fists clenched at her sides like she wanted to whop him one. Was it wrong that he was turned on?

"Relax, princess." Matt grinned. "What do you take me for? I'm not that kind of guy."

She snorted. "You're all that type of guy." Her purse strap had slipped off her shoulder, her cute summer dress was rumpled, and the carefully styled hair she'd started the day with looked as though it had come through a wind storm.

He liked it. It made her seem more approachable.

Until she spoke.

"What is *that*?" she squealed, ducking behind him and peeking around his shoulder.

Matt looked to where she was pointing and laughed outright. "That's my dog, Chewy." He bent in time to catch the hairless Chihuahua limp-racing across the tiles, its nails click-clicking to a chorus of excited yapping.

Consuela, dressed in a colorful swirly skirt and white peasant blouse with bangles jingling on her outstretched arm hurried around the corner. "Oh, Master Matt, I'm so sorry. He was eating one minute and then he was gone."

Matt tried to control the excited pooch working its way up his chest, tongue hanging weirdly out the side of its mouth and little bug eyes glittering with joy. "It's okay, Consuela, I was wondering where he was."

"It's good to have you back, your *abuela* misses you."

Matt ran a gentle hand over his pet's bony spine, flattening the narrow black strip of coarse fur that had a mind of its own. "And I missed all of you, but I'm home now, and..." He twisted his torso until Cassandra came into view, "I brought a fiancée."

Cass gave him an ugly glare, then switched on a warm smile for the housekeeper. "This is my first trip to Texas. You have a beautiful home here, Consuela."

She nodded and stepped forward to take Chewy from his arms. "Thank you, miss. The Shaughnessys are like family." She patted Matt's cheek. "This one, he is special."

Warmth for this woman, who had helped his grandma raise a troubled boy, flooded his chest. "If I am, it's because of you. I can't thank you enough for taking care of all of us over the years. And now..."

"Shh, don't talk of it, child. We don't want to invite bad spirits."

Matt smiled through the ache. He couldn't count the number of times he'd been warned about the spirits. "Yes, ma'am. I'm going to show Cassandra to her room. It's been a long day." He hugged Consuela and whispered in her ear. "It's good to be home."

He stepped back and smiled into her tear-filled eyes. "None of that now. This is meant to be a celebration."

Consuela swiped at her wet cheeks and nodded. "We will make it special. You get married here, on the ranch? Your grandmother, she's been talking non-stop about it since you called. Wait until you see her plans. It's been good for her. For all of us."

Matt winced. He couldn't believe he'd gotten himself into this mess. What started out as a simple way to please his grannie before she passed on had turned into a three ring circus. He glanced at the fuming woman beside him and wondered how long it would be before she blew the lid off this charade.

Time to find some privacy and remind her of her obligation.

"We'll discuss the wedding tomorrow." He tugged Cassandra under his arm. "My bride-to-be is swaying on her feet." He got them moving, heading down the hall toward his childhood bedroom. "C'mon, honey. Let's get you tucked in so you can get your beauty sleep."

AFTERWORD

Reviews are the lifeblood of any successful author. Without you, we can't be heard.

If you enjoy the story, please consider sharing on

your favorite social media sites, as well as GoodReads and from wherever you've bought the book.

Thank you,

Jacquie Biggar

Jacqbiggar.com

ABOUT THE AUTHOR

JACQUIE BIGGAR is a USA Today bestselling author of Romantic Suspense who loves to write about tough, alpha males and strong, contemporary women willing to show their men that true power comes from love.

She is the author of the popular Wounded Hearts series and has just started a new series in paranormal suspense, Mended Souls.

She has been blessed with a long, happy marriage and enjoys writing romance novels that end with happily-ever-afters.

Jacquie lives in paradise along the west coast of Canada with her family and loves reading, writing, and flower gardening. She swears she can't function without coffee, preferably at the beach with her sweetheart. :)

Sign up now to keep up with Jacquie's new releases, excerpts, giveaways, and more:

Newsletter

jacqbiggar.com

jbiggar@jacqbiggar.com

facebook.com/jacqbiggar

twitter.com/jacqbiggar

instagram.com/jacqbiggar

amazon.com/author/jacquiebiggar

bookbub.com/authors/jacquie-biggar

goodreads.com/JacquieBiggar

pinterest.com/jacqbiggar

ALSO BY JACQUIE BIGGAR

Wounded Hearts Series

Tidal Falls

The Rebel's Redemption

Twilight's Encore

The Sheriff Meets His Match

Summer Lovin'

Wounded Hearts Box Set

Maggie's Revenge

With This Heart

Mended Souls Series

The Guardian

The Beast Within

Gambling Hearts

Hold 'Em

Crazy Little Thing Called Love

Single Titles

Silver Bells

Missing: The Lady Said No

My Baby Wrote Me A Letter

Tempted by Mr. Wrong

Valentine: A Hearts and Kisses Romance